SCHIEF:

Askew, Distorted, Warped

Anthony DiCristofano

Contents

Prologue

Stillwater Lake reflected the glowing twilight like a mirror.

Two men drifted in a dented green canoe. Quiet. Relaxed. The kind of silence that only came after a good haul and the first couple beers.

"I'll grab the stringer," one said, leaning over the side. The metal line clinked as he pulled. Then he stopped. The fish dangled in the air—mangled. Not eaten. Not cut. Unraveled.

Flesh curled in red ribbons. One fish was split clean through the middle, not lengthwise, but wrong, as if it had folded open like a book. Bone gleamed. Skin peeled in jagged spirals.

Neither man spoke. The water beneath them held still. Then came a pop. A soft, wet sound. From below.

Two prongs pushed up through the floor of the canoe. Curved. Thick. Yellowish-white and ridged like rotting ram's horn, the ends sharp, blackened, jagged like snapped bone.

Water began to leak in around them. The older man leaned forward, whispering, "What the hell is—" The prongs twisted.

Then ripped outward, tearing the aluminum like paper. The sound was metallic, wrong, hungry. Two

1

more sickle-like claws punched through, widening the hole.

The younger man dropped through the opening up to his chest in black water. He screamed. The older man lunged and caught his arms, locking his hands around the other man's wrists. Then it hit him.

WHAM.

The canoe lurched downward, violently, like something had yanked from beneath. Water sloshed over the sides.

The man in the water screamed again, his legs convulsing under the surface.

A second hit. Harder.

The canoe bobbed down as if a giant weight had slammed into it from below. The man shrieked, eyes bulging, trying to curl up, but he was wedged in the hole. He clutched the gunwales, howling as something shredded into him.

The third blow hit like a hammer from beneath.

The canoe bucked and sagged, nearly folding as something raked up through the water and vanished just as fast.

Then stillness. No more strikes. No more sound. Just the slap of water against aluminum.

The man in the hole moaned—alive, but wrecked. His arms trembled as he clung to the gunwales, knuckles white, eyes wide and fixed on nothing. Drool and blood slid down his chin in slow rivulets. He tried to speak, but it came out as a wet rattle.

His body twitched, still jammed in the jagged opening.

The older man held his arms tight, breathing hard, staring down at him in horror. His face was gray. Sweat poured off him. He was murmuring something over and over under his breath, not even aware he was doing it.

Neither of them looked down. They didn't want to see.

He grabbed the paddle with one hand, still holding the other man's wrist in a death grip, and started rowing with awkward, jerking strokes. The canoe groaned, half-flooded, listing hard to one side People had already begun to gather. They'd heard the screams…walkers, campers, kids. Eyes wide, unsure if it was a prank until they saw the blood.

The canoe hit land. Gravel crunched. Several rushed in waist-deep to pull them out.

The injured man was gasping, pale, gripping clumps of sand. His legs were in pieces—shredded meat, bone jutting out in sick arcs, laced with lakeweed.

Some backed away. One woman dropped to her knees, whispering, "Oh my God." Then, across the lake. From the trees on the far side, something screamed. Not a wolf. Not a bird. Something else.

"SHIIIIIIIEEEFFFF—!" It rang out, too clean. Too sharp. It carried across the water like the lake wanted it to be heard. Everyone froze.

A couple of out-of-towners stood near the water, staring across the lake toward the trees where the scream had come from.

"What was that?" someone asked. No one answered. The locals knew. They just wouldn't say it. Somewhere behind them, far up the road, the distant whine of a siren began to rise.

Chapter 1: Roots of Stillwater

The Northwoods stretched endlessly, a vast green cathedral of ancient pines and birches, their tall spires swaying gently in the cool Wisconsin breeze. Stillwater Lake lay nestled among the trees, its surface smooth as glass in the early morning light, mirroring the pale sky and the slow rise of the sun. Mist hovered low over the water, curling and drifting like a restless spirit, softening the edges of the world and lending the landscape a dreamlike quality. The kind of morning that felt untouched by time, where even a breath seemed to echo in the hush.

It was a place where time moved at its own rhythm, slow and deliberate, as if the earth itself was breathing deep and steady beneath the weight of the forest. There was no urgency here, only the patient unfolding of the day, measured in birdsong and the creak of tree limbs.

Along the northern shore, a small building stood proudly despite the weathered paint and the fading wood. Schieffen's Bait & Tackle, the sign proclaimed. It had been carved by Elmer Schieffen's steady hands many years ago. The shop was simple, square and unassuming, but to those who lived around Stillwater Lake, it was a fixture, a beacon of familiarity and warmth in the heart of the wilderness. Visitors often mistook it for just another outpost, but locals knew better, it was a place of quiet rituals and old wisdom, of coffee shared before dawn and stories exchanged without rush.

Inside, the scent of pine resin and damp earth mingled with the faint musk of live minnows darting in shallow tanks. Shelves lined the walls, laden with fishing gear of every kind, hooks, lines, lures, bobbers, and other tools of the trade. The soft creak of wooden floorboards underfoot and the quiet hum of a ceiling fan were the only sounds besides the occasional murmur of customers and the laughter of children outside. There was a timelessness to the way sunlight slanted through the dusty front windows, catching motes in midair, illuminating corners stacked with old tackle boxes and jars of leeches.

Behind the counter stood Elmer Schieffen, a man whose rugged face told stories of years spent under the sun and the stars. His hands were large and calloused, the fingers strong from decades of hard work tying knots, mending nets, and handling fish. His eyes, sharp and clear, missed nothing, be it a weather change brewing or a customer in need of advice. He rarely spoke more than necessary, but when he did, his words carried the weight of someone who'd spent a lifetime listeningto the wind, to the water, to people.

But more than a bait shop owner, Elmer was the keeper of Stillwater's soul. He was a man of few words but vast knowledge, a quiet pillar of the community who knew every ripple on the lake and every whisper of the forest. Fishermen came not only for bait, but for his opinion on where the pike were biting, or for the comfort of his silent company.

At his side, or often nearby, was his only son: Corby.

Corby Schieffen was born on a misty spring morning, his first cries mingling with the soft calls of the loons on the lake. He was a boy made of the woods and water, raised among pine needles and wildflowers, where the air tasted fresh and sharp, and the land stretched wild and free. From the very beginning, the lake's rhythm became his own, waking with the sun, sleeping to the lull of waves tapping against the dock.

His earliest memories were fragments of scent and sound, a crackling campfire, the cold splash of lake water on skin, the sharp tang of pine sap, the rustle of leaves, and the distant echo of his father's deep voice telling stories. Even as a toddler, he had followed Elmer's every step with unwavering loyalty, hands outstretched toward gear too big to lift, eyes wide with the earnestness of a child trying to understand everything at once.

Mary Schieffen, his mother, had been a schoolteacher, gentle, patient, and full of quiet light. But her time was short; she died when Corby was just a toddler. Elmer carried her memory like a treasured flame, its warmth evident in the way he raised Corby with care and tenderness despite his own quiet nature.

Her photograph, faded and soft at the edges, sat in a small frame on the shelf behind the register, surrounded by fishing permits and invoices. Corby sometimes caught his father glancing at it when he thought no one was watching.

The bait shop was their home and heart, a place where Corby grew up learning the rhythms of the land and lake. He was Elmer's shadow from an early age, following his father to the dock to check nets or repair gear, sitting patiently while customers chatted or fishermen prepared for a day on the water. He learned to listen more than he spoke, to observe the flick of a fish's fin beneath the surface, or the way a line tightened in anticipation.

Fishing was more than a livelihood, it was a bond between father and son, a ritual passed down through generations. Elmer taught Corby how to tie knots, how to read the weather by the clouds, how to understand the subtle signs of fish beneath the water's surface. Each lesson was a thread weaving Corby deeper into the fabric of Stillwater.

Yet Corby's curiosity reached beyond the world of hooks and bait. Even as a small boy, he was fascinated by the mysteries hidden in the forest, the patterns on a dragonfly's wings, the way water pooled in a hollowed log, the bloom of wildflowers in spring. He collected rocks and leaves, sketched insects, and asked endless questions that sometimes exasperated his patient father. There was a hunger in him, not just for answers, but for the joy of discovering them himself.

One of Corby's favorite spots was a small clearing near the lake's edge, where sunlight filtered through the canopy and dappled the ground with golden patches. Here, he would sit for hours with a notebook, jotting observations or mixing simple potions from plants and mud. He had discovered an old science book in the local library when he was seven, a tattered volume filled with experiments and wonders that ignited a spark inside him. The book smelled of mildew and mystery, its spine broken and margins filled with scribbles from past readers. To Corby, it felt like a secret passed down just for him.

Elmer watched these early experiments with a mixture of pride and caution. "Don't go blowing up the bait shop, kid," he joked one afternoon as Corby mixed vinegar and baking soda in a jar, watching the fizzing bubbles with wide eyes. Corby had grinned, vinegar on his sleeve, cheeks flushed with excitement. "Just chemistry," he'd said, as if that explained everything.

Corby laughed, but the truth was he loved the way science could explain the magic of the world. It was a new language, one that complemented the stories of the lake and forest. A way to name the unseen forces at play beneath the surface, to understand, not just witness.

Chapter 2: Beyond the Pines

The morning sun spilled gold through the curtains of Corby's small bedroom, casting warm light on stacks of textbooks, a cluttered desk, and the faded fishing poster taped above his bed. Outside, the familiar sounds of Stillwater stirred: the distant clink of boat oars on the lake, birdsong threading through the crisp air, and the rustle of pine needles swaying in the gentle breeze.

Corby lay still for a moment, listening to the quiet symphony of the Northwoods, before pushing the covers away. Today was the first day of his senior year, a milestone that felt both thrilling and heavy with promise.

School was a modest building nestled at the edge of town, surrounded by towering pines and cracked sidewalks where wildflowers peeked through the cracks. It was the kind of place where everyone knew your name, your family's history, and sometimes your secrets. For Corby, who had grown up here and never known much else, it was both comfort and cage.

Inside, the corridors buzzed with the usual morning chatter, groups of students swapping summer stories, teasing friends, and navigating the awkward dance of teenage social life. Corby moved through the halls with a quiet confidence, his thoughtful blue eyes taking in the familiar faces: some classmates from childhood, others he had only recently met.

His closest friends, Ben, a boisterous kid with a laugh like thunder, and Grace, a shy but fiercely smart girl, were waiting near their lockers. They greeted Corby with easy smiles, slipping into the rhythms of friendship that had anchored him through middle school and early high school.

Classes rolled by in a blur of lessons and notes, but Corby's mind was often elsewhere, focused on the mysteries of chemistry. He was fascinated by the way tiny particles reacted, how bonds could form and break, transforming matter into something new. It was a world where logic reigned, rules were clear, and discovery was constant, a perfect contrast to the unpredictable wilderness outside.

Mrs. Jensen, his chemistry teacher, recognized his potential early on. "Corby," she said one afternoon, handing back a lab report, "you have a gift. Ever thought about pursuing science beyond school? Maybe college?"

The question lingered in the air, sparking a flicker of hope and hesitation. The idea of leaving Stillwater felt both exciting and daunting. Corby loved his home, the woods, the lake, but the world beyond the trees called to him with a magnetic pull.

That afternoon, after school, Corby found himself wandering down to the old wooden dock by Stillwater

Lake. The water shimmered under a pale blue sky, dotted with lazy clouds drifting toward the horizon. He sat on the edge, legs dangling, watching the ripples dance as a gentle breeze stirred the surface.

Footsteps approached, soft and familiar. Lisa Harper stepped beside him, her dark hair catching the light, eyes bright with curiosity.

"Hey," she said, settling down next to him. "Thought I'd find you here."

They had been friends for years now, neighbors who had grown up together, sharing secrets and dreams beneath these very trees. Lisa's poetry notebooks were legendary in their small town, filled with verses capturing the wild beauty and restless spirit of the Northwoods.

Corby smiled. "I was thinking about college."

Lisa nudged him gently. "You're going to go, aren't you? You belong in the city, the energy, the possibilities."

He looked out across the water, the distant hills rolling like waves of green. "Yeah. But it's hard to imagine leaving this behind."

Lisa's gaze softened. "You don't have to forget where you come from. You just have to carry it with you."

Their conversations often hovered between the comfort of home and the promise of the unknown.

With Lisa, Corby felt understood, his dreams didn't scare her, and his doubts didn't diminish her faith.

In the weeks that followed, preparations for college accelerated. Corby applied to the University of Wisconsin–Madison, choosing it for its strong science programs and its distance from Stillwater, close enough to visit, far enough to feel like a new world.

Letters arrived in a steady stream, acceptance letters, scholarship offers, orientation schedules. Each one was a step away from the life he had always known and a step toward a future full of uncertainty.

At home, Elmer remained a steady presence. The bait shop hummed with activity as the summer tourists arrived, and Corby spent long days helping with inventory, restocking tackle, and greeting familiar faces. His father's quiet pride was evident in the way he watched Corby, knowing the boy's future stretched beyond the lake's edge.

One evening, as the sun dipped behind the pines and the sky turned a deep purple, Corby and Elmer sat on the porch steps, the air filled with the scent of woodsmoke and pine.

"You've got a good head on your shoulders," Elmer said, breaking the comfortable silence. "This place will always be here. But the world's bigger than the lake."

Corby nodded. "I'm ready. It's just... hard to say goodbye."

Elmer clapped a firm hand on his son's shoulder. "You don't have to say goodbye forever. You're part of this lake, this town. No matter where you go."

That night, Corby lay awake thinking about the paths before him, the familiar trails of the forest and the unknown streets of the city. Somewhere between those two worlds, he hoped to find himself.

Lisa's words echoed softly in his mind: *Carry it with you.*

The school year passed in a whirl of tests, projects, and farewell gatherings. The small town rallied around its own, celebrating the promise of their youth even as the shadows of change loomed.

On the day of his departure, the train station buzzed with a mix of excitement and melancholy. Elmer stood tall, his weathered hands gripping Corby's backpack as the whistle blew. Lisa was there too, her eyes shining with unshed tears and unspoken hope.

"Write to me," she whispered.

"I   will,"   Corby   promised.

As the train pulled away, Corby pressed his forehead against the window, watching the trees blur into a green streak. The lake, the bait shop, the woods—all faded behind him, but not from his heart. He was stepping beyond the pines now, into a world full of promise, adventure, and the bittersweet ache of leaving home.

Chapter 3: Coming Home

Part I – The City and the Silence

The scent of coffee and melting snow clung to the air as Corby stepped out of the chemistry building at the University of Wisconsin–Madison, the late March chill catching the edge of his scarf. The campus buzzed around him, students hurrying across walkways with earbuds in and eyes down, voices echoing off brick buildings in a thousand different directions. It was nothing like Stillwater Lake.

He loved it, at least parts of it. He loved the way the city made him feel alive, part of something larger and fast-moving, like a river surging with purpose. Labs were his sanctuary; the sterile counters and precise measurements offered a kind of order that the outside world rarely did. He was good at chemistry. He understood its rhythms, its transformations. He liked that the rules made sense.

But even with academic success, and the occasional thrill of discovery, there was something missing. He felt it most in the quiet moments, walking home after a late night in the lab, or sitting in his dorm window, watching the lights from the Capitol building shimmer off Lake Mendota.

It wasn't homesickness exactly. It was more like… displacement. Like he was still walking the docks in his mind, still hearing the creak of the bait shop floorboards and the faint warble of loons calling across Stillwater Lake. That sense of *place* never left him. It just hovered, always a step behind.

Lisa's letters were lifelines. She sent them weekly, handwritten in blue ink, full of poetic fragments and snippets from home:

"The lake froze earlier this year. The pines groan when the wind pushes through, almost like they miss you too."

"Elmer keeps asking when you're coming home. He's quieter lately. Older, maybe."

"I walked past the clearing yesterday, the one we used to sit in after school. It still smells like warm moss and old sunlight."

Corby kept the letters in a shoebox under his bed, rereading them when the city noise grew too loud. Their relationship changed across the distance. It grew in some ways—more thoughtful, more intentional. But there were moments of strain too. Phone calls missed. Plans postponed. Silences that stretched too long.

He didn't doubt his love for Lisa. But the life he was building in Madison had momentum of its own. Professors encouraged him to pursue graduate school. Internships hinted at careers in biotech or pharmaceuticals. His world was expanding.

And then, one winter morning in his senior year, his phone rang. Elmer had collapsed while loading ice fishing gear for a customer.

"He's okay," Lisa said on the line, her voice tight but steady. "But it scared him. It scared me too. You should come home, Corby."

So he did.

Part II – The Return

The drive north cut through miles of snow-dusted farmland and dense pine, the roads narrowing until they became winding lanes flanked by frostbitten trees. Stillwater hadn't changed much. It never did. The lake remained frozen over, blanketed in a soft crust of snow, and the town moved at its usual unhurried pace.

Elmer was thinner, a little slower on his feet, but still sharp-eyed and stubborn. "Don't start hovering like I'm dead already," he growled good-naturedly when Corby tried to carry a bag of salt for him.

They fell into rhythm easily, father and son, side by side in the bait shop, restocking shelves and sweeping floors. The bell above the door still jingled the same way it had when Corby was six. Locals trickled in, old timers and ice fishermen who greeted Corby with wide grins and backslaps. The prodigal son had returned.

The plan was simple: stay for winter break, help out, return to Madison for the spring semester and finish strong. But something changed. The longer he stayed, the less he wanted to leave.

It wasn't just Elmer. Or Lisa, though their bond reignited quickly in shared walks and quiet dinners by the fire. It was the shop. The lake. The land.

It was watching an eleven-year-old kid light up when Corby taught him how to tie a Palomar knot. It was rebuilding the minnow tanks with a new filtration system using chemistry principles he'd studied in school. It was the satisfaction of working with his hands, solving problems that had real, immediate impact on people's lives.

When Elmer sat him down at the end of January, the offer came without flourish.

"This place is yours, if you want it," his father said, sipping black coffee in the back office. "I won't be doing this much longer."

Corby hesitated. His professors wouldn't understand. His classmates wouldn't get it. But Lisa would. And Corby... he *did* get it.

"I want it," he said.

Part III – Building Something New

Over the next year, Corby transformed the bait shop, not by changing it, but by reinvigorating it. He introduced new bait refrigeration systems and eco-friendly tackle options. He created a tiny corner for science kits and nature books for kids who, like him, once stared at minnows and wondered what made their gills move.

He kept the name: *Schieffen's Bait & Tackle*. The old wooden sign still hung proudly over the door, though Lisa insisted they add a fresh coat of paint.

They spent spring and summer evenings on the porch, watching the sky fade into lavender. Lisa had taken a job with the county nature preserve, leading tours and writing newsletters about forest conservation. She was happy. They both were.

One late July night, while stargazing near the clearing they'd claimed as teenagers, Corby reached into his pocket and pulled out a small, worn ring box. He didn't say anything at first, just handed it to her.

Lisa opened it, eyes wide, laughter bubbling up before tears followed.

"I thought you'd never ask," she whispered, and kissed him under a sky full of stars.

Part IV – The Dock

Now, a year later, Corby stood alone on the dock just after dusk. The lake stretched out before him, the surface smooth and dark like a polished stone. The wind stirred gently through the reeds. Somewhere across the water, a loon called, a long, mournful cry that echoed into the trees.

Behind him, the shop lights glowed warm through the windows. Inside, Lisa was closing up for the night, counting the register and humming one of her favorite folk songs under her breath.

Corby held a mug of coffee in both hands, the steam curling into the cool night air. He thought about how far he'd come. About the life he might've had in a lab coat and high-rise apartment. About the choice he made to return, to stay, to grow roots rather than wings. And he didn't regret it.

Stillwater hadn't changed. But *he* had. And somehow, the two were learning to meet in the middle.

The dock creaked softly beneath his boots. He looked out across the water and smiled.

Not everything needed to be explosive or grand. Some transformations, he'd learned, were quiet. Subtle. Like water carving stone.

Chapter 4: The Keeper of Stillwater

The dawn was hushed, barely more than a whisper over Stillwater Lake. Mist curled like breath over the mirrored surface, and the pines loomed motionless along the shoreline, their dark silhouettes standing sentinel as if waiting for the day to fully arrive. The old bait shop—its sign newly sanded and re-stained, caught the first golden light. "Schieffen's Bait & Tackle" gleamed quietly in the stillness, the carved letters darker than they had been, the cedar frame solid under fresh layers of varnish.

Inside, the familiar creak of the wooden floorboards echoed under Corby's boots. He moved slowly through the aisles, restocking lures, checking the tanks of live minnows, wiping down the counter with a rhythm born not of urgency but of ritual. For the first time, the keys in his pocket jingled differently, they were no longer shared. No longer held in Elmer's coat on the hook behind the door. They were his.

The official handoff had taken place just a week before. A quiet affair, like everything Elmer had done in life. No speeches, no big announcement. Just a signed title, a notary from town, and a strong handshake between father and son. Elmer had said only one thing when it was done:

"Just take care of her."

Corby had nodded, heart full and throat tight. He knew Elmer wasn't only talking about the bait shop.

Stillwater had never needed pomp and ceremony. The people around the lake understood legacy through action, through presence. When Corby quietly replaced the weathered sign with the refurbished one, the townsfolk nodded. When he reopened the shop with new shelving and a polished minnow tank, they noticed, and approved. The younger anglers asked him about bass migration. The old-timers brought coffee and stayed longer than they used to, leaning on the counter with elbows that knew their places.

Corby didn't change much. A new register, a new refrigerator for the live bait. But the hand-tied flies stayed in the mason jars, and the dusty map behind the counter, marked with generations of secret fishing spots, remained untouched. He kept the radio tuned to the same classic station Elmer always played. Progress, but not betrayal.

And Elmer? He watched from the porch most mornings now, coffee in hand, wrapped in the same old flannel jacket no matter the weather. His steps had grown slower in the past year, his voice softer. At first Corby had chalked it up to age, the natural wear of time on a man who had carried more than his share. But by the first frost, even Elmer couldn't deny something deeper was wrong.

"It's just breath," he'd muttered one morning, pausing halfway to the truck with a wheeze. "Can't seem to get it in all the way these days."

A trip to the local clinic confirmed it wasn't just breath. It was his heart. Enlarged. Irregular. Fragile.

The diagnosis landed like an anchor in Corby's chest. Elmer didn't protest the pills, didn't argue when Lisa, now living full-time in a rented cabin nearby, started helping with meals. But the quiet resignation in his eyes said more than words. He'd seen too many winters. He knew the count.

Corby shifted into caretaker without thinking. Mornings started earlier, nights ran later. He balanced orders, deliveries, and paperwork with doctor's appointments and quiet walks down to the dock. Sometimes, in the softer moments, they would sit side by side on the porch as loons called from the far side of the lake.

"You know," Elmer said one evening, his voice raspier than usual, "your mother would've liked what you've done with the shop."

Corby said nothing, the weight of the moment a pressure in his chest.

"She always thought you'd go off to some big lab, maybe wear one of those white coats. Said you were too bright for worms and leeches." A ghost of a smile crossed Elmer's face. "Guess you proved her wrong and right, didn't you?"

Corby chuckled softly. "Maybe."

They watched the lake turn gold with the setting sun. Elmer's hand, worn and veined, reached out and patted his son's knee once. No more words were needed.

Chapter 5: The Silence Between the Trees

Winter came early that year. The first snowfall dusted the lake in October, clinging to the evergreens and outlining each branch in icy filigree. Stillwater slowed, wrapped in white and quiet, the kind of hush that seeps into the bones of the forest and stays there.

Elmer grew quieter with the snow.

He slept more, read less. The worn flannel blanket never left his lap. He no longer made it to the shop porch in the mornings, and Corby stopped pretending to expect him. Instead, he brought coffee inside, sitting with his father at the kitchen table while the lake turned to ice behind the frosted windows.

"Cold's settling in early," Elmer murmured one morning, eyes distant.

Corby nodded. "Yeah."

"I always liked the quiet," Elmer said. "Most people don't. Makes 'em nervous. But I liked it. Felt... honest."

That was the last real conversation they had.

Elmer passed in his sleep two weeks later. No struggle. No sound. Just the slow stilling of a body that had weathered storms and seasons, that had stood like a pine through it all, until it didn't.

Corby found him at dawn, sitting upright in the armchair, blanket tucked around his legs, a half-read book facedown on his lap. He didn't cry at first. He made the calls. He told Lisa. He sat on the porch while the wind picked at the edges of the lake and let the stillness pour over him.

The funeral was small.

A scattering of neighbors, old fishing friends, townsfolk who remembered Elmer as the man who could fix anything, find any lure, and always offer the right kind of silence when someone needed it. The pastor from the Lutheran church read a Psalm, and Lisa read a short poem she'd written the night before. Corby stood without speaking, a folded flannel shirt in his hands, and placed it gently on the closed pine casket before they lowered it into the ground behind the chapel.

There were no eulogies. No slideshow. Just the soft thump of earth and the rustle of pine needles overhead.

Afterwards, people came back to the shop for coffee, just like they always did. They brought casseroles and jars of jam, hand-written notes and small envelopes with cards. They told quiet stories about Elmer, how he'd once helped an old man who'd fallen in the woods, how he used to sharpen knives for free, how he'd always remembered a child's name.

Lisa lingered beside Corby as he listened. He barely spoke. Just nodded, smiled faintly, poured coffee. She knew better than to force anything.

That night, when everyone had gone and the wind had picked up, Corby stood alone inside the bait shop. The radio played softly in the background, some slow country song that Elmer liked, more steel guitar than lyrics. He walked to the back counter, ran his hand along the edge, and sat down on the stool his father had favored.

The shop smelled the same. Earth, fish, and old wood. But it felt different. Not heavier, exactly, just quieter. Emptier. More his.

He reached into the bottom drawer and pulled out Elmer's ledger. The one with decades of inventory, sketched fish, half-finished orders, and scribbled notes in the margins. The last entry had been from over a month ago.

Corby added a new one that night. Not just numbers. Words.

Elmer gone. Took the morning with him. Shop feels like the lake in winter. Still, but not dead. Just waiting.

He closed the book and turned off the lights.

Chapter 6: The Spring Thaw

Spring came late. The ice cracked slowly on Stillwater, groaning and shifting like an old memory loosening its hold. Then, all at once, the thaw arrived. The lake shed its frozen skin and opened to the sun again. Loons returned, calling across the water. Ducks nested in the reeds. Life resumed.

Corby stood at the edge of the dock one morning, hands in the pockets of a faded jacket, watching the mist rise in soft curls from the surface. It was the first time in months that the lake looked alive again, and he realized how much he had missed it, missed its voice.

In town, people still greeted him as "Elmer's boy." Some habits were hard to break. But at the shop, something had shifted. The sign still read *Schieffen's Bait & Tackle*, but the hands behind the counter were new. His. The rhythm had changed. The heartbeat was different.

He began small.

Repainted the trim. Reorganized the shelves. Moved the ice chest closer to the register. Stocked new types of lures after noticing a demand from visiting anglers. And in the back, behind the counter where Elmer had kept his ledger, Corby cleared out space for something new.

He kept the old books, the wooden ruler, the spare glasses, and a photo of Elmer holding up a monster pike from years ago. But he also brought in jars of labeled samples, plant matter, small bones, soil types. He hung a periodic table next to the fish chart. On the desk, a small microscope. An idea had taken root.

Stillwater's kids often wandered in after school, as Corby had once done. He started showing them things, how to test water quality using strips, how different bugs indicated the health of a lake, how to identify the minerals in a rock. At first, it was just curiosity. But slowly, it grew into something more.

One afternoon, a boy named Mason asked, "Is this still a bait shop or a science lab?"

Corby smiled. "Both."

He began offering Saturday morning "explorer days" for local families, short nature walks, a lesson on ecosystems, a bit of fishing. It wasn't a rebranding. It was a deepening. A way to honor what had come before and invite in what could come next.

Lisa stood by him through it all. She'd taken a teaching job in the next town over, driving in each day and returning by dusk. They talked late into the night, about curriculum, about poems, about legacy and loss.

"You're doing what your dad did," she said one night, sitting beside him on the dock. "Keeping the lake. Just… in your own way."

Corby nodded. "Sometimes I hear him. Not like a ghost or anything. Just, when I'm measuring the water temperature or fixing a reel, I can almost hear him say something. Like he's still in the rhythm of it."

"You're the rhythm now," Lisa said gently.

One morning, Corby stood on the dock again, same spot, different man. The mist curled over the lake just as it had the morning he returned from college. But now the stillness felt full, not empty. Like breath held, not lost.

In his pocket was a small leather notebook, its pages half-filled with ideas: education programs, ecology projects, partnerships with state parks. Dreams once tied to city streets now rooted deeply in pine needles and lake water.

He looked toward the shop, its windows warm with the morning light, a flicker of movement inside as Lisa unlocked the front door for him.

"Okay, Dad," Corby whispered into the breeze. "It's ours now."

Then he turned and walked up the dock, each step sure, the future unfolding in the soft creak of wood beneath his feet.

Chapter 7: Fading Currents

As time wore on, a slow breath settled over Stillwater Lake, warm and steady, but heavy with something unspoken. The Northwoods still stretched endlessly, towering pines reaching skyward in patient silence, but the lake itself no longer sang its old familiar song. The water, once shimmering with the promise of abundant fish and endless summer days, had grown quieter. A faint murmur beneath the surface whispered of change, something shifting, fading, unraveling.

Corby Schieffen stood behind the counter of Schieffen's Bait & Tackle, the worn wooden floor creaking softly beneath his boots. His fingers traced the edges of the latest ledger, the ink of the numbers stark and unyielding: profits down again. For three years now, the steady income the shop once enjoyed was shrinking like a fading shadow. The summer tourists who once flocked to the lake had started to find other destinations. Fishermen, fewer in number, cast lines into waters that no longer promised the bounty they once delivered.

He sighed, the weight of the numbers sinking deep into his chest. The shop was his inheritance, a legacy passed down from his father, Elmer, a man whose life had been etched into every corner of the place. Yet now, without Elmer's steady hands and calm voice, the shop felt vulnerable, exposed to a world that seemed to be slipping away.

The scent of pine resin still clung to the walls, mingling with the faint musk of bait and the sharp tang of lake water. Shelves stood stocked with lures and lines, but the customers were fewer. The soft murmur of voices, once a constant hum of community, had thinned to a sparse echo.

Outside, the lake stretched wide and still beneath a pale sky. The surface, usually bustling with boats and laughter, held only a scattering of small craft. The water no longer teemed with life; the once abundant fish seemed to have vanished or moved on.

Corby's gaze drifted to the dock where a lone heron stood, motionless and patient, waiting for its prey. The bird's stillness mirrored his own conflicted heart. He thought of Elmer, whose large, calloused hands had built and maintained this shop with a quiet pride. Elmer had passed two years ago, leaving Corby the full responsibility of their family's legacy. Often, Corby imagined what his father would say about these changing times.

"Keep your head up," Elmer's voice echoed in memory. "The lake's been through hard times before. It'll come back."

But Corby wasn't so sure. The signs of decline were all around, the water's clarity had diminished, patches of algae bloomed earlier each year, and the fish populations had dropped noticeably. Environmental experts had visited on occasion, speculating about pollution, shifts in climate, and overfishing. Corby listened, absorbing their warnings with a sinking feeling. The forces at work were vast and unknowable, much larger than any one man or bait shop.

His worries extended beyond the lake to the business itself. Expenses crept higher each year. Repairs, supplies, and upkeep gnawed at his savings, even as income fell short. Corby had been steadily setting money aside, dreaming of building a home for himself and Lisa, a new beginning beyond the modest cabin they shared. But with profits waning, those dreams began to feel more fragile.

Lisa Harper was the light in the growing gloom. She was bright and restless, full of warmth and hope that sometimes felt almost contagious. They had been inseparable since their youth, their lives intertwined like the roots of the ancient pines that surrounded Stillwater. She wrote poetry in battered notebooks, capturing the wild beauty and restless spirit of their home. Her faith in the future was steady, a tether Corby clung to in moments of doubt.

On many summer evenings, they sat together on the weathered porch of the bait shop, watching the sun bleed colors into the lake's horizon.

"I want us to have roots here," Lisa said softly one night, her hand finding his. "No matter what happens, this place is ours."

Corby squeezed her hand, the warmth steady and reassuring. But inside, uncertainty churned. The weight of responsibility pressed down on him. The shop was more than a livelihood, it was a symbol of his family, their history, and his identity. To see it falter felt like a fracture in the foundation of his world.

Despite the quiet despair creeping in, Corby refused to give up. He was resourceful and determined, searching for ways to breathe new life into the shop. He experimented with promotions, offering guided fishing trips in partnership with local guides, trying to attract younger customers with newer, trendier gear, and even considering diversifying inventory to include camping supplies and outdoor apparel.

Yet, the challenges persisted. The town itself was changing. Younger generations were leaving for the bright lights of cities like Minneapolis and Chicago, seeking opportunity far beyond the Northwoods. The community was shrinking, its tight-knit fabric fraying at the edges.

One chilly autumn afternoon, Corby stopped by Mae's Diner, a small gathering place where locals shared news and swapped stories over strong coffee and homemade pie. He found Ben, his longtime friend, nursing a cup and staring into the steam.

"Business slow?" Ben asked, nodding toward the bait shop as Corby settled beside him.

"You could say that," Corby replied, rubbing his forehead. "Three years running, and it's only getting worse. The fish just aren't here like they used to be."

Ben shook his head. "People say the lake's changed. I heard about the algae bloom last summer, and some say it's pollution from upstream. Hard to say for sure."

Corby's stomach tightened. The lake was the heart of everything here, if it was sick, then what hope was there for the community?

The conversation turned toward memories, of better days when the docks overflowed with fishermen, and the shop was alive with laughter and chatter. It was a reminder of what once was and what might be lost.

That night, Corby walked home beneath a sky heavy with stars. The cool air was thick with the scent of pine and woodsmoke, but the usual chorus of frogs and insects was subdued, a quiet that seemed to echo his own thoughts.

Lisa met him at the cabin's door, her smile warm but eyes shadowed with concern.

"We'll find a way," she whispered.

"I want to believe that," Corby said, pulling her close. "But it's getting harder every day."

Their future loomed uncertain, he was eager to build their dream home, but the strain of the failing

39

business made each step feel heavier. Corby wrestled with the balance between hope and reality, knowing that the choices he made now could shape not only his life but the fate of the shop that was his family's legacy.

As the leaves turned and winter whispered its approach, Corby found himself standing at the edge of the lake more often, searching for answers in the water's surface. The fish were fewer, the visitors rare, but the lake's quiet strength remained. Somewhere beneath the fading currents, the pulse of Stillwater endured.

And Corby was determined to find it again.

Chapter 8: Storm on the Horizon

Autumn arrived on a gray wind, sweeping cold and uncertainty through the Northwoods. The seasons turned, leaves burned gold and crimson before falling to the earth, and Stillwater Lake, once a mirror to the sky, seemed to reflect the growing turmoil in Corby's heart.

Corby moved through his days like a man caught between worlds, the boy who had dreamed beside these waters and the man now forced to confront their stark reality. Each morning, he unlocked the bait shop with a mixture of hope and dread, as if the worn door itself might finally refuse to open.

Business was no longer just slow; it was fragile, hanging by threads worn thin by time and circumstance. Tourists had dwindled to a handful of loyal regulars, and locals who still fished arrived less frequently, their own lives pulled away by new jobs, families, and cities that promised brighter futures. The lake's once bountiful fish population continued to decline, and whispers about environmental damage grew louder, though solutions seemed far beyond Corby's reach.

Late one October afternoon, Corby sat behind the counter, staring at the empty registers. Lisa entered quietly, her face pale but determined. She had just returned from the town meeting, one where the community discussed the lake's decline and the threat it posed to their way of life.

"They're talking about restrictions on fishing licenses," she said, lowering her voice as if the walls might hear. "They want to limit the number of fishermen to help the lake recover."

Corby felt a cold knot tighten in his stomach. If fewer fishermen were allowed, what hope was there for the bait shop?

"We'll have to adapt," he said, forcing calm into his voice. "Maybe focus on other outdoor gear, or even start renting boats. We can't give up yet."

Lisa nodded, but the worry in her eyes betrayed her faith.

That evening, as the chill crept through the cabin, Corby sat alone, the weight of the future pressing down. The dreams of building a home with Lisa, of a family raised beside these waters, felt more distant than ever.

Money was tight. Bills piled up, and the savings meant for their new house dwindled with each passing month. Corby worked longer hours, pushing himself to the brink, but it never seemed enough.

He thought often of his father, Elmer, steady, resilient, a man who never let the storms break him. Corby tried to summon that same strength, but the strain was relentless.

Lisa remained his anchor, offering support even as she wrestled with her own fears. They clung to each other in the quiet nights, sharing whispered hopes and silent tears.

The community around them also felt the strain. Friends moved away, shops shuttered, and the familiar rhythms of small-town life grew faint. Stillwater was changing, and Corby feared it might never return to the vibrant place he once knew.

Yet, beneath the hardship, a stubborn flame of hope burned. Corby vowed to fight for the shop, for the lake, and for the future they dreamed of. The storm was fierce, but he would weather it, no matter what it cost.

Chapter 9: Cracks in the Ice

The winter of 1975 settled over Stillwater like a heavy blanket, muffling the world in gray and white. Corby found himself walking a lonely path beneath barren trees, the cold air biting at his cheeks but unable to chase away the chill inside him. The bait shop was shuttered for the season, but the weight of its troubles followed him everywhere.

Days blurred into nights in a haze of worry and exhaustion. The steady rhythm of the Northwoods, once a balm for his restless spirit, now felt like a slow, relentless ticking clock counting down to an uncertain end.

With profits falling deeper into the red, Corby's frustration grew. He began drinking earlier in the evenings, a cheap whiskey from the local store becoming his unwelcome companion. It was a small escape, a brief numbing of the sharp edges that life had become. But the relief was fleeting, and the darkness it masked crept back in stronger.

Lisa watched with growing alarm as Corby withdrew into himself. Their once easy laughter and quiet conversations had dwindled to tense silences and sharp words. The dreams they shared, of a new home, of a future built together, felt further away with each passing day.

One evening, after a particularly long day spent trying to untangle the shop's dwindling orders and mounting bills, Corby stumbled into the cabin, the cold night air trailing behind him. Lisa was waiting, the warmth of the small stove doing little to thaw the distance growing between them.

"You're drinking again," she said quietly, her voice cracked with exhaustion and worry.

Corby's jaw tightened. "I'm handling it. Better than sitting here worrying all the time."

"It's not handling it," she said softly, tears welling in her eyes. "It's running from it. From us."

He looked away, shame and anger twisting inside him. "I'm doing what I can."

"But it's not enough," Lisa whispered. "We're losing each other."

The room seemed to close in around them, the silence heavier than words. For the first time, Corby felt the full weight of what was slipping through his fingers, not just the business, but the love and hope that had once felt unbreakable.

Outside, the wind howled through the trees, rattling the cabin windows like a ghostly reminder that the storm wasn't over.

In the weeks that followed, Corby's drinking grew more frequent. His temper flared unpredictably, and the steady support Lisa had once offered wavered under the strain. They argued more, their fights punctuated by moments of painful regret and desperate apologies.

Friends in town noticed the change too, the man who had once been a steady pillar now seemed fractured, weighed down by invisible burdens. Some offered advice, others gave space, but all watched with quiet concern.

One bitter night, Corby sat alone in the dark bait shop, the flicker of a single bulb casting long shadows. The shelves, once vibrant with promise, now felt empty and abandoned. He cradled a glass of whiskey, staring at the faded photographs on the wall, memories of his father, of simpler times, of a future that now seemed like a distant dream.

The cold seeped into his bones, but the cold inside was worse, a deep ache of failure, loss, and fear.

And yet, despite the growing cracks, a small voice inside him refused to give up. Somewhere beneath the weight of his mistakes and despair, the embers of hope still glowed, fragile but alive.

But to hold onto that hope, Corby knew he would have to face more than just the storm outside, he would have to confront the storm within.

Chapter 10: A Dangerous Experiment

Corby slammed the battered door of the bait shop behind him, the echo bouncing off empty shelves like a taunt. The bitter wind whipped through the cracked windowpanes, chilling the room and deepening the hollow ache inside him. He dropped his coat on a rickety chair and lit a cigarette, the smoke curling upward like the tangled thoughts swirling in his mind.

The repossession notice for his car still lay on the counter, a cruel reminder of just how far things had fallen. Bills were piling up, property taxes, overdue payments for supplies, all threatening to drown him. The nights blurred together in a fog of whiskey and frustration, each one a little darker, a little lonelier than the last.

Lisa's worried face haunted his dreams, her pleas to stop drinking falling on deaf ears. But Corby felt trapped in a spiraling vortex, helpless to pull himself back. The bait shop that had once been his family's anchor now felt like a sinking ship, and he was its reluctant captain.

In the dim corner of the shop, the minnows darted nervously through the water in their tanks, their silvery scales catching the faint glow of a flickering lamp. It was here, in this cramped makeshift lab behind the storage room, that Corby clung to the last flicker of hope. His chemistry background, once a distant memory, had become an obsession. He spent hours tinkering with a mixture of nutrients and growth stimulants, a concoction pieced together from old textbooks and half-remembered formulas.

The first trials had been promising. Minnows exposed to the mixture grew larger, more active, and produced more offspring. Tanks once sparse now teemed with life, a small victory amid the encroaching darkness.

Yet with every small success came a gnawing fear. The lake outside was a fragile ecosystem, a delicate balance shaped by generations. Introducing foreign chemicals could have disastrous consequences. Still, the bait shop was bleeding money, and the fish population was dwindling fast. Without change, there might be no future left.

One cold evening, as the wind howled outside and the minnows swam energetically in the glass tanks, Corby's thoughts darkened. What if the mixture could be released into Stillwater Lake? Could it replenish the fish, bring back the anglers, and breathe life into the struggling community? Could it save the bait shop, and maybe even his future with Lisa?

The idea terrified and exhilarated him.

Corby drained his glass and wiped the sweat from his brow, the weight of responsibility pressing down hard. This was no longer a simple experiment, it was a gamble with everything on the line: his livelihood, his home, the lake itself.

Lisa's voice echoed in his mind, a fragile warning against reckless ambition. But Corby's anger and fear drowned out reason. He was a man pushed to the edge, clinging to a fragile hope in the face of relentless loss.

The mornings came cold and gray. Light seeped weakly through the thin curtains of the bait shop's small office, casting long shadows over cluttered papers and half-empty coffee cups. Corby sat slumped at his desk, eyes bloodshot from sleepless nights and too many drinks. The faint hum of the cooler was the only sound, broken occasionally by the splash of minnows in their tanks nearby.

He reached for his notebook, pages filled with hastily scrawled notes and chemical formulas. His secret sanctuary, the place where hope and desperation tangled.

But with every passing day, the lines between them blurred. His drinking grew heavier, the nights darker. Arguments with Lisa frayed the quiet fabric of their home, silences stretching longer, sharp words replacing tenderness.

One evening, she found him mixing chemicals at their kitchen table, frustration clouding his eyes.

"Corby, this has to stop," she said quietly, voice trembling. "You're losing yourself. We're losing each other."

He looked at her, the woman he loved, and felt the crushing weight of failure pressing down like a stone.

"I'm trying," he whispered. "I'm trying to save us. Save this place."

But even as he spoke, doubt lingered in his mind. Was he playing God with nature? Could he control what he had unleashed in those tanks?

The nights grew colder. The shop quieter. Fresh bills piled up. Phone calls from creditors came more frequently. The gnawing fear that everything was slipping through his fingers never left.

Yet somewhere deep inside, a stubborn spark of hope remained. The question was how long that spark could survive before it was snuffed out entirely.

Chapter 11: Into the Dark

The bait shop was cloaked in silence, broken only by the soft, steady tick of an old clock perched crookedly on the peeling wall. Outside, the night pressed close, cold and still, thick with the chill of early autumn that bit through the thin walls. Corby sat alone in the shadowed backroom, the single lamp casting a weak circle of light that trembled like a fragile flame against the darkness creeping in from the corners.

In his hands, he cradled the small glass vial, the chemical solution he had painstakingly concocted, the culmination of desperate nights spent scribbling notes and mixing compounds. The liquid inside shimmered faintly in the lamplight, a silent promise that was both hope and threat.

Corby's mind was a storm of conflicting emotions. Shame curled at the edges of his thoughts, a slow-burning guilt that whispered how far he'd fallen. This was not the way his father would have run the bait shop, steady, honest, rooted in tradition. But desperation gnawed deep, clawing at his resolve and drowning out reason. Bills piled up like dark clouds, Lisa's voice haunted him with worry and fear, and the future he had dreamed of building together now felt like slipping sand.

Yet beneath the shame was something sharper, fiercer, a stubborn ember of pride, a hard-earned sense of control. For the first time in months, maybe years, Corby felt like the master of his own fate. Not a victim of circumstance, not a man beaten down by the slow death of the lake and the shop. Tonight, he could decide what happened next.

His eyes flicked to the tanks in the corner, where minnows darted through the water like tiny sparks of life, unnaturally large and fast, their numbers growing each day. They were his secret triumph, the proof that the chemical worked. But would the lake itself, the vast, fragile ecosystem that had been the heartbeat of Stillwater, survive such interference?

The thought brought a stab of anxiety, sharp and cold as the night air seeping through the cracked windows. What if he was playing God? What if the lake rejected his gift and turned against him? What if this gamble destroyed everything?

Corby's breath hitched, and he drew a shaky hand across his face. His fingers trembled—not just from the cold, but from the weight of the choice ahead. Every instinct screamed to hold back, to wait, to protect the legacy his father had left him. But every fractured hope whispered to act, to fight back, to take the chance.

Hours crawled by in slow, oppressive silence. He wrestled with his thoughts, memories, and fears, the faces of customers who no longer came, the quiet dinner table where Lisa sat in silence, the empty spaces in the shop where laughter once lived.

When the clock's ticking finally faded into the deep stillness of midnight, Corby stood, a new resolve settling over him like armor. He slipped into his worn coat, its fabric stiff with cold and age, and tucked the vial deep into his pocket.

Outside, the world was a shadowed landscape, the skeletal trees outlined against the ink-black sky. The chill wrapped around him like a second skin, cold and biting, but Corby felt a strange clarity amid the frost. Each step toward the lake was a step away from helplessness, from defeat.

At the dock, the lake lay silent, an endless mirror reflecting the void above. The water was still, almost sacred in its quiet, untouched by the storms brewing in his heart. Corby knelt at the edge, the cold biting through his gloves and biting into his skin. He pulled the vial from his pocket and held it over the water, the liquid inside catching the faint moonlight.

His pulse thundered in his ears. Shame tugged at his soul, the fear of consequences pressing hard against the thrill of control.

With a slow, deliberate motion, he uncorked the vial and poured the chemical into the lake's dark embrace. The liquid spread in faint ripples, almost invisible at first, then drifting outward like an unseen tide.

Corby stayed there long after the last drop had vanished beneath the surface, watching the stillness reclaim its hold. The cold seeped deeper into his bones, but his hands were steady.

Turning back toward the bait shop, his breath clouded in the frosty air. His heart was heavy, weighted with regret, hope, fear, and a fragile sense of triumph.

He was a man at a crossroads, standing alone between the past he had lost and the uncertain future he might yet shape with his own hands.

The lake was no longer untouched.

And neither was he.

Chapter 12: The Waiting Season

Corby stood behind the counter of Schieffen's Bait & Tackle with a stiff cup of coffee in his hand, his eyes fixed on the lake. The steam curled upward into the cold morning air, much like the slow churn of thoughts in his mind. He hadn't slept the night before, not really. Every creak of the floorboards, every gust of wind against the windows, had sounded like an accusation.

It had been five days since that midnight walk.

Five days since he'd stood ankle-deep in the frozen shoreline, breath misting in the air, and watched the rippling surface of Stillwater Lake swallow gallons of his homemade compound. The sky had been black as ink, stars hidden behind a heavy curtain of cloud. He hadn't used a flashlight, just the thin silver light of the moon and his memory of the path.

His hands had trembled then, not from cold, but from the magnitude of the act. He'd knelt at the water's edge and whispered, almost as if in prayer, as he tipped the jugs into the shallows. The mixture dispersed with a slow swirl, vanishing into the vast unknown.

When it was over, he'd stood there for a long time, unsure if he felt ashamed or proud. Maybe both. It had been his decision, his risk. No more waiting for miracles. No more clinging to fading legacies.

Now he waited for the lake to answer.

He peered through the frost-rimmed window. The lake looked the same as it always had, still and vast, its surface broken only by a few scattered ice flows and the distant movement of birds. There were no signs of disaster. No floating fish. No chemical slicks. At least not yet.

Corby sipped his coffee, the bitterness grounding him.

He hadn't told Lisa. He didn't know how. Their conversations had become more like quiet negotiations than the affectionate banter they once shared. She still came by the shop from time to time—mostly to bring groceries or check on him—but there was a distance between them, thick as fog. She hadn't moved out, but she may as well have. They spoke little, touched less.

Still, she hadn't left. That was something.

It wasn't until two weeks later that he noticed the change.

It started with a local named Vern Tiller, an old-timer who came in every Saturday morning for waxworms and a bag of beef jerky. Vern had shuffled into the shop with more pep than usual, his face ruddy with cold and a strange, boyish excitement.

"Caught me a monster up by Black Pine Point," he said, plunking a photo onto the counter. "Look at that brute!"

Corby blinked at the picture. A northern pike, at least thirty-five inches, maybe more, held awkwardly in front of Vern's flannel coat. He hadn't seen one that size come out of Stillwater in years.

"Damn," Corby muttered. "What were you using?"

"Just a plain ol' red-and-white spoon," Vern said, shaking his head. "She hit like a train."

Corby forced a smile, his heart thudding behind his ribs.

More stories followed. In the days that came, other regulars stopped by with tales of better-than-average catches, perch in impressive clusters, bass bigger than usual.

Still, something was happening.

Business ticked upward. Slowly, at first. A few more tackle boxes sold. Minnows cleared from the tanks faster than he could restock. Word began to spread beyond Stillwater, especially after the *Ashland Gazette* ran a short column titled **"Stillwater Lake: A Hidden Gem for Spring Fishing?"** with a grainy photo of a local teen hoisting a fat crappie and grinning like he'd won the lottery.

Tourists began to trickle in.

Corby watched it all unfold with cautious hope. He dared not believe the improvement was real, but day by day, the shop took on more life. The register rang more frequently. People lingered longer. The once-still air of the shop now buzzed with chatter and laughter again.

He cleaned the place, fixed the sign, even replaced a few broken rods from the display. For the first time in months, he worked late not because he was avoiding life, but because there was work to do.

Lisa noticed. She commented on it one evening over dinner, a modest plate of venison stew eaten in the silence of their living room.

"You look… better," she said. Her voice wasn't warm, but it wasn't cold either.

Corby met her eyes, unsure of what to say. He didn't tell her why. He couldn't. Not yet. But he nodded and managed a quiet, "Thanks."

Their conversations remained brief, but something fragile had begun to shift. Less tension. Less silence. It wasn't a recovery, not by any stretch. But it wasn't the freefall it had been.

Still, guilt followed him like a shadow. He knew the success of the shop was built on a secret that could unravel everything. There were nights when he woke drenched in sweat, heart pounding, imagining fish floating belly-up or the lake turning green with algae. But so far, there had been no signs of damage—only improvement.

Perhaps, he told himself, he'd gotten it right.

Perhaps his experiment wasn't just an act of desperation, but a stroke of brilliance.

He began keeping records in a notebook again. Measurements, conditions, observations. It helped him stay grounded, made him feel like a scientist again instead of a drunk chasing luck. He even toyed with refining the formula, adjusting the ratios, planning for a more targeted application in case things ever turned again.

But beneath the cautious optimism was something darker. A seed of unease he couldn't shake.

Because deep down, Corby Schieffen knew he'd crossed a line.

And once you cross it, there's no going back.

Chapter 13: Beneath the Surface

The bell above the door jingled, sharp against the hushed stillness of the morning. Corby looked up from his ledger, pencil tucked behind his ear, a mug of lukewarm coffee balanced between his hands. Business had held steady for the past few weeks, brisk enough to keep the lights on, just enough to breathe.

The man who entered was unfamiliar. Tall, broad-shouldered, with weathered hands and a DNR jacket zipped halfway up. His eyes, a piercing gray, scanned the shop like he was measuring its worth.

"You Corby Schieffen?" he asked, voice low and flat.

"I am," Corby said cautiously.

The man stepped forward, pulling a laminated ID from his coat. "Greg Talbot. I work with the Department of Natural Resources. We've been getting some... curious reports from the Stillwater region."

Corby's pulse quickened, a ripple of cold tightening in his chest. "What kind of reports?"

Talbot pulled a small notebook from his pocket, flipping to a dog-eared page. "Unusual fish specimens. A muskie with translucent skin caught just outside Big Tooth Bay. A perch with four dorsal fins. Bass with distorted jaw structures, larger than normal, almost canine in appearance. Some of the anglers think it's a fluke. But it's more than one report."

He paused, letting the weight of his words hang in the air. "Anything strange going on out here?"

Corby forced a casual shrug, though his throat had gone dry. "Not that I've seen. Folks say a lot of things when they're excited about a big catch."

Talbot studied him for a beat too long. "Sure. Just figured I'd ask."

He left a card on the counter and gave a polite nod before slipping back into the cold, the door thudding shut behind him. The silence that followed was deafening.

Corby stood there for a moment, heart pounding, the paper card staring up at him like an indictment.

That night, he lay awake in the narrow bed he still shared with Lisa, though they barely touched anymore. The shop had grown busier, yes. Revenue was up, the shelves were restocked, and even Lisa had seemed to soften a little. But now—now the cracks were showing.

And worse: they pointed back to him.

He pulled himself from bed and padded down to the shop in the dead of night, barefoot and hollow-eyed. The minnows in the tanks darted nervously as he flicked on the overhead light. They looked normal. Healthy. Active. But his eyes couldn't stop searching for something, an extra fin, a too-sharp eye, some sign that the mutation had begun at the source.

His notebook sat on the counter, full of his early notes. Dosages. Projections. Half-baked equations scrawled in weary handwriting.

He flipped to a page where he'd sketched out the original compound's chemical structure. His chest tightened as he read it now, realizing how much of it was guesswork. How much had been fueled not by science, but desperation.

He had known it wasn't stable. Had told himself it was temporary. Had promised himself the dosage was small.

Had lied to himself all the same.

The next morning, the phone rang just as he opened the shop. He recognized the voice, it was Vern Tiller again, the one who'd caught that monster pike weeks ago. But his tone now was less triumphant and more… confused.

"Corby," Vern said slowly. "I pulled a catfish this morning that had teeth. Not just sharp ones, molars. Like human ones. Ever seen anything like that?"

Corby's hand gripped the receiver too tightly. "Can't say I have. Must be a deformity."

"Yeah. Maybe. But I've been fishing this lake for forty years. I ain't never seen anything like it."

He hung up. More calls followed that week. A teenage girl posted a photo of a sunfish with three eyes to the Stillwater community board. Another man claimed he'd reeled in a trout that hissed before it died.

Corby laughed that one off to nerves or exaggeration, but it still kept him up that night.

The newspaper that had once touted Stillwater as a hidden gem now ran a headline that sent a chill through Corby's bones:

"Mutant Fish in Stillwater? Locals Report Strange Catches"

The article stopped short of blaming anyone. But the subtext was clear: something was wrong in the water.

Lisa found the article on the table one morning, her eyes scanning the page in silence.

"You know anything about this?" she asked softly.

Corby hesitated for a fraction of a second too long. "No," he said. "People talk."

She looked at him for a long moment before sliding the paper away and walking to the sink. The air between them thickened, more silence, more distance.

The shop stayed open. Business was still good…for now. Tourists were intrigued by the "monster fish" rumors. Some even came looking for the strange catches. But the locals were wary. Old-timers muttered about curses. A few regulars stopped coming altogether.

Corby watched it all with a heavy mix of dread and inevitability. The potion had worked—undeniably. But it had also done… something else. Something irreversible.

The lake had changed. And deep down, so had he. He knew he couldn't undo what he had done. But he also knew this wasn't over, not by a long shot.

The surface of Stillwater was calm. But beneath it, things were shifting.

And soon, the real consequences would rise.

Chapter 14: The Fallout

The morning sun filtered through a hazy film of frost clinging to the shop windows, but it brought no warmth. Corby stood behind the counter of Schieffen's Bait & Tackle, arms crossed over his chest, staring at the empty parking lot outside. Not a single truck. Not a single boat trailer. The gravel lot that once buzzed with anglers was still and silent.

He hadn't rung up a sale in five days.

The phone no longer rang with curious calls about record-breaking fish. Now it rang with accusations, or worse, complete silence. People had started avoiding him altogether. Even the regulars who used to linger for coffee and local gossip stopped showing their faces. Stillwater Lake had become a place of whispers, and his shop had become a ghost.

The fish were dying.

One by one, they washed up on the shoreline, bloated bass, trout with glassy, bulging eyes, catfish with strange lesions and translucent skin. At first, Corby told himself it was a bad algae bloom. Then he blamed runoff, or warming water temperatures. But in the back of his mind, he knew the truth.

He had poisoned the lake.

And it had poisoned everything else in return.

The night Lisa left was as quiet as snowfall.

She stood at the doorway of the small cabin they had once dreamed of turning into a home. A single suitcase rested by her feet. She wore the coat her mother gave her, and her eyes, so full of quiet sorrow, held no more anger. Only exhaustion.

"I can't do this anymore," she said.

Corby sat hunched on the edge of the bed, clutching a half-empty bottle like it was the only thing left keeping him steady. "You don't have to go," he said, voice hoarse. "It's just a bad stretch. Things'll turn around."

Lisa didn't flinch. "You made a choice, Corby. And now it's swallowing you whole. You don't talk to me. You don't even look at me. I've been sleeping next to a ghost."

He opened his mouth to respond, but the words didn't come. There was nothing left to say that hadn't already been said a hundred different ways in a hundred different silences.

"I'm going to stay with Marla. In Milwaukee," she said gently. "At least for a while."

He didn't walk her to the car. He just sat there, listening to her footsteps grow fainter. When the engine finally started and the headlights swept across the trees, he didn't move. He stayed in the dark, clutching the bottle, staring at the wall as though it might tell him what to do next.

The shop remained open in name only. Corby still unlocked the door every morning, but it was ritual, not hope. No customers came. The minnow tanks were nearly empty, algae creeping along the glass. Even the minnows had stopped thriving. The miracle he'd engineered had died with the lake.

Bills went unopened. The phone went unanswered. The refrigerator buzzed constantly, as if reminding him that something inside was still alive, even if he no longer felt it.

He spent most of his days in the back room now, the makeshift lab where all of it had started. It was the only place he could still pretend to be in control. Vials, tubing, beakers scattered across the table like abandoned prayers. His notebooks had become more chaotic, filled with sketches, calculations, question marks scrawled with increasing desperation.

He had stopped trying to fix the lake. Now he was trying to understand what he had done. What had gone wrong. What had mutated. He recorded the changes in the fish, tracked patterns, wrote formulas that blurred into nonsense. Some nights he sat in front of the tanks and talked to the fish, the way a man might confess to God.

Outside, the first signs of fall began to touch the trees. Leaves turned amber and red, then let go. The lake, once teeming with laughter and splashes, now lay cold and still, like a wound that refused to heal.

Occasionally, he would walk down to the water's edge, a flask in one coat pocket, a field notebook in the other. He'd stare out across the surface, watching for movement, hoping for a sign that maybe, just maybe, things would right themselves.

But the lake was quiet. Too quiet.

One evening, as the sun dipped low and the trees cast long, skeletal shadows, Corby stood ankle-deep in the water, staring down at his reflection. He didn't recognize the man looking back. Hollow cheeks. Tired eyes. A stranger built from guilt and stubbornness.

He splashed water on his face and whispered, "I didn't mean to."

It was the first time he said it out loud.

But there was no one left to hear.

Chapter 15: Breaking Point

The bait shop sat beneath a heavy gray sky, its worn wooden siding sagging under the weight of years and neglect. Inside, dust motes floated through slanting shafts of pale light, settling on counters cluttered with forgotten fishing gear and empty bottles. Corby moved silently through the shadows, a ghost trapped in his own life, weighed down by failure and isolation.

The air was thick with the sour tang of stale beer and spilled dreams, a mixture that hung over the room like a curse. The once-bright tanks of minnows, carefully tended in better days, now stood murky and half-forgotten, their tiny occupants few and listless. The laughter and chatter of customers were distant memories, replaced by an oppressive silence that pressed down on Corby's chest.

Months had passed since Lisa had left, since she'd quietly packed what she could and disappeared into the noise of Milwaukee, seeking refuge from a life that was unraveling too fast. Their fights had shredded the fragile threads holding their relationship together, each harsh word deepening the wound until only cold, strained silences remained.

Now, Corby was alone, and the solitude was a slow poison. He found himself caught in a spiraling storm of anger and despair, anger at the dying lake, the mutated fish, and most bitterly, at himself. The man who had once dreamed of saving the bait shop with his chemistry knowledge was now consumed by what his desperation had wrought.

His refuge was the bottle. The fridge, long emptied of cold beer, the floor housed few empty cans of PBR, and the nearly empty whiskey bottle sat on the bench like a cruel reminder of lost hope. Tonight, the weight was unbearable. Corby's hands trembled as he reached for the vial containing the last remnants of his secret chemical formula, the mixture that once seemed like salvation.

Corby uncapped the vial with shaking fingers, the faint smell of chemicals mingling with the stale smell in the air. His gaze drifted to the small wooden table where remnants of his lonely dinner sat, a frozen pizza half-eaten, its cardboard box stained and forgotten. Beside it lay the cleaver, its edge dulled from years of use but still sharp enough for its grim purpose.

His mind roiled with a chaotic blend of fury and despair. The world outside seemed to mock him, the fading light through the cracked windows cast long shadows, as if the very walls whispered of his failures. He raised the vial to his lips, the liquid burning as it slid down his throat, a bitter fire igniting in his chest.

A strangled scream tore from him, raw and ragged, echoing through the hollow shop. The pain surged like wildfire, mixing with the storm of emotions that overwhelmed him, rage at the world, anguish at his lost love, resentment toward nature itself for refusing to bend to his will.

Stumbling, Corby looked down at his ring finger. The finger that would never wear the ring of his lost fiancé. In a fit of fueled fury, Corby seized the cleaver from the table. His vision blurred as tears and anger clouded his mind. Without thinking, he brought the blade down hard.

The cleaver bit deep into his hand, sending a burning sensation that spread instantly. Corby's scream was raw and desperate, echoing through the empty bait shop. His eyes blurred with tears and sweat as pieces, his thumbs, pinky, and ring fingers, fell scattered across the worn wooden table, stained with blood that pooled dark and thick like spilled ink.

For a moment, the world seemed to freeze. Corby's breath came in ragged gasps as he stared at the bloody mess, disbelief and horror crashing into him with overwhelming force.

Suddenly, a knock at the door shattered the silence. Corby tensed, gripping the cleaver tightly as if it were his last lifeline.

"Corby? It's me, Jim. Open up, man," the familiar voice called, worried and gentle.

The door creaked open, and Jim stepped inside, his eyes widening in shock at the scene, the scattered fingers, the blood-stained table, and the raw, fragile remnants of Corby's shattered hand.

"Corby… your fingers…" Jim whispered, horror and confusion thick in his voice.

Corby's lips curled into a bitter, unsettling smile. "Fingers? Those are bait," he spat, his voice laced with madness and denial.

His laughter burst out, wild and broken, echoing off the cold walls before snapping suddenly into angry screams, sharp and filled with anguish.

Staggering toward the wood-burning stove, Corby grasped it with blood smeared hands, twisting it away from the chimney. The stove hissed against his skin, blood steam and hot smoke filling the cramped room, thick and suffocating.

Corby's grip tightened around the hot stove, his breath ragged as the burning smoke stung his eyes. The room seemed to close in around him, a suffocating trap of his own making. His wild laughter turned to desperate screams, echoing off the cracked walls of the bait shop.

Jim stepped closer, his face pale but resolute. "Corby, please, let me help you."

But Corby's mind was unraveling, the chaos inside him spilling over. With a sudden, frantic motion, he hurled the stove across the room. It slammed into the battered wooden wall, sending embers and sparks flying like tiny stars.

The fire caught quickly, licking greedily at the dry wood, filling the shop with a thick haze. Flames curled and twisted, devouring the remnants of Corby's shattered dreams, the empty shelves, the battered counters, and the tiny minnow tanks that once held his fragile hope.

Jim stumbled back, coughing, his heart pounding. "Corby, get out of here!" he shouted, voice cracking with fear.

But Corby was already moving, clothes aflame and smoke swirling around him as he staggered past Jim. The agony and madness fueled his steps as he ran toward the lake, the cold night air hitting his burning skin. Without hesitation, he plunged into the dark, cold water, the flames from the bait shop blazing behind him like a funeral pyre.

Jim stood frozen on the shore, the crackling fire behind him and the ripples fading where Corby disappeared beneath the surface. Frantic, he scanned the dark lake, but there was no sign—no splash, no struggle. Corby's body was swallowed by the night and the cold, leaving only silence in his wake.

The fire consumed the bait shop, casting a fiery glow into the sky as emergency crews arrived too late to save the building or their old friend.

Chapter 16: The Vanishing

The morning after the fire, the town of Stillwater woke under a heavy gray sky. The bait shop's skeleton sat blackened and smoldering against the pale light of dawn, a jagged scar etched into the lakeshore. The air was thick with the smell of smoke, the acrid scent curling into the trees and settling in the cold, damp earth.

From the edges of the crowd gathered near the ruins, whispers floated, shaky and uncertain, like the flicker of fading hope. Corby was gone. No sign of him in the rubble. No sign of him in the lake. Just a silence so profound it seemed to press down on everyone's chest.

The sheriff moved quietly among the neighbors, his face grim but composed. Soon, a team arrived, boats, nets, divers, and search crews from the county, ready to scour Stillwater Lake inch by inch. The water, once a source of life and laughter, now seemed ominous and endless.

They dragged the lake for hours, then days. Divers plunged into the cold depths, their movements slow and deliberate, searching for any hint of Corby's presence beneath the surface. Nets were cast again and again, the water disturbed only to settle back into its silent expanse. But nothing came up. No trace of Corby.

No proof that he had truly passed in the chaos of flames and water.

The town held its collective breath. The fire had taken the bait shop, the heart of their community, but it had also taken their friend, their brother, their anchor, and yet, it had left no answers.

At the diner, the talk was low and uneasy. The regulars shared stories of Corby, his stubbornness, his laughter, his dreams, and his demons. Some recalled the old days when the lake brimmed with fish and life, others spoke in hushed tones about the strange things that had begun happening before the fire: the mutated fish, the dwindling crowds, the creeping sense of something unnatural lurking beneath the surface.

"Maybe the lake didn't want him," one fisherman muttered, staring out at the still water. "Maybe it took him back."

A few nodded, swallowing their coffee as if trying to gulp down the unsettling thought.

Meanwhile, the sheriff's department fielded questions from reporters and worried townsfolk alike. How could a man disappear so completely? How could the lake offer no clues? No evidence that Corby had survived, or perished?

The mystery gnawed at the community. For a man who had been so entwined with the land and water, the bait shop and its visitors, Corby's sudden vanishing was like losing a part of Stillwater itself.

Lisa's closest friends worried about her, urging her to move away, to find peace somewhere else. She resisted, holding onto the fragile hope that Corby might somehow return, or that the truth would surface in time. She found herself wandering by the lake's edge, eyes scanning the gray waves for a sign, anything.

But the lake offered nothing.

At night, she dreamed of Corby, his smile, the sound of his laughter mingling with the rush of waves. Then the fire, the screams muffled by the water, and the terrible silence that followed. She would wake trembling, the darkness pressing close.

Meanwhile, the town struggled to move forward. The bait shop ruins stood as a stark reminder of better days, the dreams that had burned away with Corby's disappearance. Fishing trips slowed, and the community that had once thrived on the lake's bounty felt the loss ripple through every family.

The mystery of Corby's fate became a whispered legend, a question passed down over campfires and at kitchen tables, how does a man disappear without a trace, leaving only the lake's depths to guard his secret?

Chapter 17: Shadows by the Lake

Stillwater's nights had always carried their own quiet magic—the gentle rustle of pine needles, the distant call of loons, the soft ripple of water against the shore. But in the months since the fire and Corby's disappearance, the nights had taken on a different tone. A chill that no autumn breeze could explain, a weight pressing down on the small town like a gathering storm.

It started subtly at first. A flicker of movement just beyond the tree line near the burnt-out shell of the bait shop. Locals passing by on late drives would catch glimpses of something large and awkward, too tall to be an ordinary man, too uneven in its gait to be any animal they knew. The figure was always hunched, moving slowly, almost deliberately, vanishing before anyone could get a good look. People whispered among themselves, nervously laughing it off, but there was unease beneath the bravado.

At first, no one spoke openly of it. After all, the town was still reeling from the shock of Corby's sudden descent into madness and the flames that had consumed the shop. The loss was raw, personal. Yet the sightings began to multiply. Reports came in of strange, lumbering shapes crossing the back roads late at night, always retreating quickly into the dense woods. Drivers swore they'd seen eyes reflecting in the darkness—too large, too wild to belong to any known creature.

One evening, Old Man Harris, a lifelong resident who had never feared the woods, confided to the local diner crowd. "I heard somethin' down by the lake," he said, voice low. "Like... moanin'. Not like any animal I ever heard. Like a soul caught between worlds." The others exchanged uneasy glances. Stories like that were usually dismissed as drunken ramblings, but Harris had always been reliable.

More disturbing were the sounds drifting through neighborhoods. A sobbing, sometimes almost a whisper, sometimes a guttural moan carried by the wind. People reported hearing it just outside their windows in the dead of night. When they'd rush to look, the yard was empty—only the shaking leaves and a sudden coldness remained.

Children stopped playing near the lakeshore after dusk, and even the fishermen who'd braved the cold waters to keep their livelihood now stayed away, unwilling to face whatever lurked in the shadows. A few brave souls tried to shine flashlights toward the woods, catching only fleeting movements that vanished before the beam could settle.

Rumors grew like wildfire. Some said Corby had never truly left, that his spirit haunted the burnt remains of the bait shop, restless and angry. Others whispered of curses, of nature's wrath unleashed for tampering with forces better left alone. The older generation shook their heads, blaming youthful superstition and grief for fueling these tales. Yet no one could deny the creeping dread that seeped into every quiet moment.

Town meetings were held, mostly out of nervous habit, to discuss the strange happenings. The sheriff assured everyone there was no threat, that they'd increase patrols and investigate sightings. But the reports never stopped. If anything, the frequency seemed to grow in the darkest hours before dawn.

In the dead of night, when the world fell silent, some swore they could see flickering shadows moving near the water's edge, figures too tall, too misshapen, too wrong to belong to any living being. The boundary between the natural and the unnatural felt thin, fragile.

And Stillwater, once a haven of calm, now held its breath beneath the looming darkness, waiting for what might come next.

Chapter 18: The Hollow Hours

The bus rolled into Stillwater just as the sun was slipping beneath the horizon, bleeding soft pink and orange into the sky. Lisa stepped down, her movements slow, weighed down by a tiredness that no amount of sleep could shake. Annie and Mark were waiting at the station, their quiet smiles a fragile lifeline in a world that felt suddenly fragile and unmoored.

"You're home," Annie said gently, reaching out to steady her. But the word 'home' landed like a stone in Lisa's chest.

She hadn't come back for comfort. She'd come back to the ashes, the empty spaces where dreams had once taken root, where Corby's laughter had once filled the air. The bait shop, the lake, the cabin, all etched into her memory like a story ending too soon, pages ripped away before the final chapter.

The town had changed, or maybe it was her. The weight of the loss, the shock of his absence, and the ache of what could never be anymore pressed down on her chest with every breath.

Inside Annie's cozy kitchen, light spilling warm and golden, Lisa sat quietly, tracing the rim of her tea cup with fingers too numb to feel. She tried to hold back the wave of grief, the steady flood of memories, of promises whispered in the dark, of plans sketched in hopeful scribbles, now turned to dust.

Annie's voice cut through the silence, soft but steady. "You've been through so much. It's okay to feel lost."

Lisa nodded, a thin smile flickering briefly, but her eyes stayed distant, staring out at the darkening world beyond the window, at a lake that held so many ghosts.

The quiet stretched between them, thick with what remained unsaid. The future was uncertain, the past a wound still fresh and raw. Lisa felt the exhaustion settle deep into her bones, not just from the travel, but from the heavy burden of coming home to nothing.

"You're just tired," Annie said as she refilled Lisa's cup of chamomile tea, her voice warm and low. "You've been through a lot."

Lisa nodded, grateful, but unconvinced. Yes, there had been the trauma, the fire, the disappearance, the town's whispers thick as smoke in her ears. Yes, the travel had been long. But this... this was something different.

It was as if Stillwater itself had reached out with invisible fingers, wrapping around her mind, her bones, her lungs. The town had changed in her absence. Or maybe it hadn't. Maybe it was her that had changed, peeled open by grief and left too raw to return.

They sat in the kitchen of Annie and Mark's modest home, a long cabin nestled near the southern pines just a mile or so from the lake's edge. The windows were fogged slightly with the autumn chill, and soft yellow light spilled from the overhead bulbs, casting long shadows on the hardwood floor.

Mark tried to keep the mood light. He made her laugh once, showing off a ridiculous dance he'd taught their golden retriever, Boone. Annie kept refilling her cup, brushing Lisa's hair back from her face like an older sister.

"We've got you," she said softly. "Just rest tonight. The room's already made up."

Lisa gave a thin smile, the kind people give when they want to say thank you but can't find the energy to mean it.

That night, the guest room felt like a cocoon. The walls were a soft forest green, the bed firm but comfortable, layered in handmade quilts that smelled of lavender and something older, cedar, maybe. Outside, wind brushed through the trees in slow, deliberate sighs.

She lay still for a long while, staring at the ceiling where the shadows of the fan blades turned slowly like ghostly clock hands. Sleep was an uphill climb, her body aching with the weight of too much feeling and not enough rest. But slowly, steadily, the world softened. Slowly, steadily, the world softened. Her thoughts scattered like dry leaves, and the bed cradled her with quiet warmth, drawing her down into the fragile embrace of sleep.

Then the sobbing began.

At first, it slipped into her dream like a radio left on in another room. A low, breathy sound—fragile and human. A voice, just at the edge of hearing. Lisa dreamed of water. Of standing knee-deep in the lake, holding Corby's notebook, its pages soaked and bleeding ink.

The sobbing grew louder. Choked. Gasping. Closer.

She stirred. The dream fractured. For a moment she wasn't sure where she was—back in the cabin, alone in Milwaukee, somewhere between memory and nightmare.

Then her eyes opened.

The sobbing hadn't stopped.

Lisa lay frozen in the dark, breath shallow, ears straining. It was real, or real enough. Not inside her head. Not now. The sound came from somewhere close, too close. As if someone were weeping just on the other side of the bedroom wall.

And then, it faded.

Bit by bit, like breath dispersing into fog. No sudden silence, just a slow unraveling, the way sorrow sometimes slips away when it's too tired to stay.

She closed her eyes again. Told herself it was a dream lingering at the edge of wakefulness. That's all.

Then came the footsteps.

A long, heavy drag. Then a thump. Wood creaked under weight. A dragging step again. Then another.

She bolted upright, covers falling away in a heap. "Annie?" she called, her voice hoarse.

No answer.

"Mark?"

This time she heard movement down the hall. Doors opening. Muted voices. Then Annie's voice, low and shaking: "We heard it too."

Lisa stepped into the hallway, pulling a shawl around her shoulders. Together they moved to the kitchen, drawn by the same unease that pressed on their lungs like low altitude.

The kitchen window faced the back porch. Beyond the glass, only the porch light glowed—a dull, amber ring encircling part of the deck. The rest was blackness. Trees hunched like watching figures.

Mark was already standing at the back door, his hand gripping the knob. At his feet, Boone stood stiffly, ears pricked, tail frozen. The dog's whole body leaned toward the door, silent but electric with tension.

And then it came.

A scream.

Not human. Not animal.

It split the night like a blade.

A high-pitched screech, metallic and guttural all at once, so loud Lisa felt it in her molars. Boone barked—just once, then lunged forward as Mark opened the door.

The dog burst out into the night, paws thundering across the porch boards, then into the grass beyond.

For a moment, they could see him, his sleek body moving through the weak golden ring of light cast by the porch lamp. But with every stride, he moved further into the black. The light didn't stop, exactly, it *thinned*.

Boone's tail flicked as he reached the edge of that invisible threshold. Then his outline began to waver.

His fur dimmed to gray, his form flickering like static. The light clung to his back for a moment, just the curve of his spine glowing faintly, then vanished as if devoured by fog.

Echoing back from the darkness, they heard Boone's low, fierce growl snap into a sudden, crushing bite—hard and unrelenting.

Then a loud, sickening sound pierced their ears and souls, a splintering snap, like bone breaking. Boone let out a short, staccato yelp, a final cry, before silence swallowed the yard whole.

Lisa's breath caught. The porch light flickered once, hesitated, then steadied.

Annie grabbed Lisa's hand, fingers trembling. "What... what the hell was that?"

No one answered.

The light from the porch flickered, just once, a subtle flutter in the bulb like a heartbeat skipping.

Lisa peered into that opaque curtain beyond the porch. Her eyes strained for any sign of Boone, a flash of fur, a glint of movement, anything. But the darkness didn't move. It only watched.

And then... a new sound.

Something *wet* shifting.

A slow, dragging sound—like something heavy being pulled through leaves and gravel.

Mark stepped back inside and shut the door gently, slowly turning the lock. Not that a lock would matter. Whatever was out there, if it wanted in, it would not be stopped by a knob and a deadbolt.

No one spoke.

The dragging sound faded.

And then...

Silence.

Not the usual kind.

The *unnatural* kind. Where even the insects stopped. Where even the trees refused to rustle.

The kind of silence that knows you're listening.

Lisa stepped back from the door, her breath catching in her throat. Her vision swam slightly, exhaustion pulling at her, grief wrapping itself around her bones like ivy, and now this... this fear, ancient and animal, flaring hot in her gut.

"What did Boone see?" she asked, her voice cracking.

Mark didn't answer. But his knuckles had gone white around the edge of the countertop, gripping it like a man trying to ground himself.

"It's not just the lake," Annie whispered. "It's the woods too."

"No," Lisa said. "It's *him*."

They all turned to her.

She didn't mean to say it. The words had tumbled out like something shaken loose in a dream. But now that they were in the air, they rang with certainty. With something too close to truth.

Mark moved to the hallway closet and pulled down a heavy-duty flashlight. Then, without a word, he turned and crossed to the corner cabinet—one with a lock that had long since become a formality. From it, he retrieved his old bolt-action .30-06 hunting rifle.

This was the Northwoods of Wisconsin. Everyone had a rifle. Everyone knew how to use it.

He slid the bolt open with a sharp, practiced motion, thumbed in a handful of rounds from a battered green box, then racked the bolt closed with a final, metallic *click* that echoed through the kitchen like punctuation.

Annie flinched at the sound. Lisa didn't.

Lisa didn't respond. Her gaze was fixed on the door. On that fading porch light. On the place where

Boone had disappeared, where sound had twisted into horror and left only silence behind.

She didn't say it aloud, but something deep inside her knew.

Annie paced near the sink; arms crossed tightly over her chest. The flashlight sat on the kitchen table next to the rifle, casting faint reflections in the window glass. Lisa didn't take her eyes off the dark beyond the porch.

"We should wait for morning," Annie said softly, more a wish than a plan.

But Mark was already dialing.

The call to the sheriff's office was brief. Sheriff Kaelton didn't ask many questions, he just said he'd be there in twenty minutes with Deputy Strom, and that they'd bring their own lights and weapons. In Stillwater, strange calls in the middle of the night weren't new anymore. What *was* new was the edge of silence that followed each one.

When they arrived, the red and blue of the cruiser lights bled into the fog, staining the trees in brief pulses of color before vanishing again behind the mist.

The night had grown thicker, wetter. The air hung heavy with moisture, so dense it felt like breathing through cotton. The porch light could barely push beyond the railing now, and every flashlight beam scattered in the fog like it was hitting milk glass.

As they moved into the backyard, the beams formed halos, ghostly, shifting rings that shimmered and danced with every step. Trees became silhouettes, looming and half-formed. Shadows moved that didn't belong to any of them.

Lisa stayed close to Annie, her borrowed boots muffled in the thick grass, her breath fogging in the chill. Mark took the lead, rifle held steady, flashlight strapped to the barrel. Sheriff Kaelton flanked him, his own shotgun at the ready. Strom brought up the rear, a younger man with jumpy eyes and a too-tight grip on his pistol.

The dog's tracks were still visible, deep paw prints in the soft earth, headed straight toward the woods.

Mark whispered, "This is where we lost him."

The fog churned slightly, as if disturbed by their voices.

A wind picked up, gentle, almost warm, yet it carried a foulness that had no place in the clean woods. A subtle rot, like old meat left in the sun. Sheriff Kaelton wrinkled his nose.

The beams of light fanned out across the trees. And that's when they saw it.

Not   Boone.   Not   a   body. But **marks**.

Along one of the pine trunks, deep gouges, parallel and uneven, raked into the bark by something large.

Strom stepped closer, his breath fogging in front of him.

"That's fresh," he said.

Lisa stared up at the trees. The fog made the branches blur into nothingness, into a ceiling of vague white. She had the sudden and unwelcome thought that something might be *above* them.

The beams flickered again, more severe this time. Lisa's flashlight blinked twice, then steadied.

Sheriff Kaelton turned in a slow circle, his shotgun tracking the light.

"No sounds. No owls. No insects. No nothing," he muttered. "Just like at the lake."

Mark stepped carefully to the edge of the woods. The trees loomed ahead, still and patient, their limbs swallowed by mist. His flashlight swept the ground— and caught.

Something.

Tangled in the roots of a fallen pine lay Boone's collar.

He crouched down slowly. The thick leather was torn, not chewed but *ripped*, as if it had been caught in something that pulled until it gave way. The brass name tag was bent almost in half, the engraved letters warped beyond reading.

Beside it, nestled in the moss and mud, were clumps of golden fur, tufts torn loose, some matted with dark, tacky blood.

Mark picked up the collar, turning it over in his hand. His breath came shallow; eyes fixed on the smear of red across the inside of the strap.

As they stared at the shredded collar in hand, the Sheriff called out. Everyone's gaze dropped again to the spot near the fallen tree, now illuminated by the Sheriff's flashlight. A faded scrap of fabric tangled in damp moss and roots. It was rough and threadbare, a fragment of blue and gray plaid, stained and worn as if forgotten by time.

But that was not all.

Nestled against the cloth, half-hidden beneath rotting leaves, was a lump. Small. Misshapen. Soft, but not like a stone or a clump of mud. The pale greenish-yellow surface glistened under the trembling light, a slick, sickly patch that oozed faintly with moisture.

Lisa swallowed hard. The scent hit her next, a sharp, sour tang, like decay fermented in the wet earth. Something alive in its own dead way.

She edged back a step, eyes wide and frozen. The others drew closer, voices hushed.

Mark shifted, his rifle trained on the shadowed trees beyond. Kaelton knelt, bringing a gloved hand toward the object, but carefully, as if it might snap or lash out.

"It's not... animal," Kaelton said, voice low and rough. "That's flesh. Human."

Lisa's breath caught. The piece was about the size of a baseball, but mangled—skin mottled with patches of slick, jelly-like substance peeling at the edges. Coarse hair clung to one side.

The group fell silent. The fog seemed to thicken, folding over them like a shroud.

Strom whispered, voice barely audible. "This is bad. Real bad."

Kaelton sealed the fragment in a plastic bag, the squelch of wet tissue muffled but unmistakable. The smell seemed to follow them even as they backed away.

The flashlights spun their ghostly circles as they walked in silence back toward the safety of the porch, the oppressive presence lingering like a breath on the back of their necks. Crossing beneath the faint porch light, Lisa glanced once more at the dark woods before stepping back in. The door closed behind them with a slow creak, and the world seemed to hold its breath.

Inside, no one spoke. Not yet. The house felt smaller somehow—its walls closer, its corners darker. The scent of the woods clung to their clothes, bitter and metallic.

Lisa sat at the edge of the couch, her hands clenched in her lap. The others moved around her in small, quiet ways, Mark unloaded the rifle, Annie making tea no one would drink. Her suitcase was still upstairs, half-unpacked. She'd planned to stay for a week. To rest. To try and feel normal again.

But that was before.

Now, the thought of sleeping here, of waiting out another night, made her stomach turn. The silence no longer comforted. It listened. It *watched*. Tomorrow, she would leave. No goodbyes, no explanation. Just the road. Just distance. She only had to make it to morning.

Chapter 19: First Sighting: Pine Hollow Campground

The sun was dipping low behind the pines when the group arrived at Pine Hollow Campground. Three couples and a few singles, all from Illinois, eager to trade the relentless noise and concrete of the city for the quiet embrace of the woods. They set up tents on soft mossy ground, the scent of pine thick in the air, mingling with the faint smell of damp earth and fallen leaves.

As twilight slipped into night, the group gathered around a crackling fire. The smell of grilled brats mingled with smoky wood and fresh earth, while laughter and easy chatter floated through the clearing. Bottles of beer passed between hands, and the radio played softly nearby, filling the spaces between the quiet rustle of leaves and the occasional hoot of an owl. The night felt alive but calm, a perfect escape from their hectic lives.

Then, suddenly, slicing through the peaceful chorus of the woods, came a scream, sharp, sudden, and unlike anything they had ever heard. It was a chilling sound, carrying an eerie mix of desperation and pain that hung in the cold night air.

Heads snapped toward the direction of the noise. Conversations dropped off mid-sentence. Unease settled over the group like a heavy fog. Some exchanged uncertain looks, others tried to laugh it off.

"Probably a coyote or something," Greg said, trying to steady his voice and force a laugh. "We're here for nature, right? That's just part of it."

The scream echoed again, longer this time, a high-pitched wail that seemed to stretch far into the darkness. It didn't sound like any animal they had heard before. The rawness of it sent a shiver through their spines.

Still, the group forced themselves to relax, telling stories and passing around more beer to drown out the unease. Gradually, people drifted away from the fire, one by one retreating to their tents. The fire's glow flickered against the towering pines as silence reclaimed the clearing.

But the scream returned, piercing the night with a terrifying shrillness that clawed at their senses. It was a sound that seemed almost human, a desperate, drawn-out cry that rose and fell like the wind, but with a haunting edge no one could explain.

Those left near the dying fire exchanged anxious glances, the atmosphere now thick with tension. They pulled their jackets tighter, trying to shake the feeling that they were being watched, that the woods held something waiting in the shadows.

As they finally slipped into their tents, the screams continued, echoing over the still waters of the nearby lake, a chilling lullaby for a restless night.

Sometime after midnight, when the last embers of the fire had long gone cold and the woods had slipped into a breathless stillness, a couple stirred in their tent. A sharp *crack*, the unmistakable snap of a twig underfoot, cut through the silence and woke them both.

Jason opened his eyes first, his breath catching in his throat. He nudged Sierra beside him, who blinked groggily in the dark. They both listened. For a moment, all was still again, only the faint rustle of trees shifting in the breeze, the distant lapping of the lake. They almost dismissed it, thinking maybe it was a deer or raccoon.

Just as Jason began to relax, ready to drift back into sleep, it came again, this time not a twig, but a sound. A low, gurgling moan.

Sierra sat up, her eyes wide, blanket clutched to her chest.

"Do you hear that?" she whispered.

Jason nodded slowly, lips pressed tight. It sounded *almost* human, a strange mix of groaning, moaning, and what could only be described as choking. Phlegmy. Mucus-thick and guttural. Each breath sounded like it had to claw its way out of a swamp of fluid.

Grrrrrrhhhk... hhhhkkkgggghh...

Then came the footsteps, slow, deliberate, and *dragging*.

Sierra covered her mouth, stifling a gasp. Jason instinctively reached for the flashlight beside their bedroll, but didn't turn it on.

A faint shadow began to creep across the canvas of their tent wall. It moved in time with the dragging steps, growing slowly larger as the source approached from behind what had been their fire pit. The shape was... *off*. Hunched and heavy, the arms long, too long, swinging in a slow, deliberate arc.

Sierra whispered, "A bear?"

Jason shook his head, staring at the silhouette. "That's not a bear," he muttered.

The shadow wasn't rounded and lumbering, it had a sort of spindly posture, the kind that didn't match anything native. It was too upright... but malformed.

The moaning stopped.

Silence hung over the tent like a held breath.

Then — a *wet splatter*. Something hit the outer wall of the tent — liquid, thick in its fall. It began to pool slightly above the zippered entrance, then ran in fat droplets down the side like melting candlewax.

Jason didn't dare move.

Then, an abrupt and rapid scratching began against the tent wall, sharp and relentless. Within seconds, the fabric shredded and tore away, collapsing in a heap on the ground. As they looked up, frozen in horror, the dark figure loomed above them. Its long, sinewy arm stretched high overhead, ending in two unnaturally long appendages—the index and middle fingers, curved yet extended like blades. At the tips, something sharp gleamed, resembling knives or talons.

The couple was so paralyzed with terror they couldn't scream. The figure seemed to hesitate, as if contemplating whether to bring those sharp talons down upon them. It trembled and shook, caught in the terrible moment between threat and uncertainty.

Jason's fingers shook as he groped blindly for the flashlight, his heart pounding so loudly he feared it might give them away. Finally, his hand closed around the cold metal cylinder, and with a desperate flick, a narrow beam of light pierced the oppressive darkness. The beam landed squarely on the towering figure looming just beyond the tent's torn fabric, illuminating its grotesque form in harsh, unforgiving detail. Both he and his partner froze, paralyzed by a mixture of terror and disbelief as the full horror of what they were facing was cruelly revealed in that harsh glow.

Its mouth hung open, moist and glistening in the flashlight's beam, lips stretched unnaturally wide to reveal a ghastly sight. The tongue inside was clearly visible, but one side was melted away, frayed and raw, as if scorched or torn by some terrible force. The teeth that framed the gaping maw were rotting, jagged and unevenly spaced, with dark gaps between them where decay had taken hold. The sight sent a cold shiver down the spine, a visage so grotesque it seemed almost unreal, like something ripped from the darkest corners of a nightmare.

His long hair hung in tangled, matted strands, wild and unruly as if it hadn't felt a brush or care in months. The gusts of cold night wind whipped through it, sending the ratted locks twisting and whipping around his gaunt face like dark, restless shadows. Strands clung damply to his forehead and cheeks, streaked with grime and something darker, hinting at long neglect and hardship. The chaotic movement of his hair only added to the eerie, unsettling presence he projected in the flickering light.

His skin was thin and translucent, stretched tight over his skeletal frame like fragile parchment. The pale, almost ghostly surface revealed the boney structure beneath, every ridge and contour sharply defined as if the flesh itself had receded. Beneath that fragile layer, other darker shapes writhed and twisted—perhaps blood vessels, swollen and tangled like dark threads pulsing faintly in the dim light. The unnatural visibility of these unseen workings beneath the skin gave the figure a haunting, otherworldly appearance, as if the very essence of life was struggling just beneath that fragile membrane.

His flesh was marred by countless small holes, irregular and disturbing in their pattern. Some of these holes were barren and empty, like dark, silent scars etched into his skin. Others writhed with grim life, writhing worms or parasite. Their slow, twisting movements visible. It was as if his body had become a host to a hidden, grotesque world, a place of decay and infestation that blurred the line between living flesh and rot.

What remained of his shredded clothing hung in tatters, soaked and heavy, clinging desperately to his gaunt frame. The fabric, torn and stained, pressed against his skin like a second, suffocating layer, slick with moisture that glistened faintly in the dim light. Beneath the ragged cloth, his body was unnervingly thin, yet powerfully muscular, every sinew and tendon standing out sharply, like twisted ropes under thin pale skin. His frame, though lean, radiated a disturbing strength, as if honed by endless hardship and unnatural strain, each movement taut with raw, animalistic strength and tension.

One of his ribs had a compound fracture and protruded through the skin. The opening wept and the end of the bone was black and rotting.

In the moment the harsh beam of the flashlight cut through the darkness and struck his pale face, the creature's gaping mouth opened wide, releasing a raw, deafening scream that tore through the still night air like a banshee's wail — a chilling, drawn-out cry of "Schiiiiiiiiiiieeeeeeeeefffffffffffeeeeee" that echoed off the surrounding trees and sent a shiver deep into the bones of anyone unfortunate enough to hear it.

Sierra, frozen beneath the weight of terror, lay rigid on her back inside the shredded remains of the tent. Her wide eyes reflected the flickering beam of the flashlight, still locked on the grotesque figure towering above them. The scream—"Schiiiiiiiiiiiieeeeeeeeeeffffffffffeeeeee"—rattled through her like electricity, leaving her nerves frayed and her thoughts scattered. Her hands clutched the fabric beneath her as if it could anchor her to the waking world. But the fear, thick and absolute, pressed in until her mind could no longer bear it. Her eyes rolled back, her limbs went slack, and she passed out cold, still as stone beneath the silent weight of the nightmare looming above her.

Jason barely had time to register Sierra's collapse beside him. The moment her body went still, a fresh jolt of panic surged through him. The scream still rang in his ears, sharp and piercing, as if it had etched itself into the air around them. He turned his flashlight back up toward the creature, toward whatever had once been a man.

Its long limbs twitched in the beam, and for a heartbeat, Jason thought it might strike. But it didn't. It just stood there, trembling violently, its ruined form rippling with uneven breath. Jason couldn't move. He couldn't think beyond the primal instinct screaming in his head to protect Sierra, to escape, to survive.

He felt warmth spreading down his thigh and realized, dimly and with a strange detachment, that he'd lost control of his bladder. The fear had overwhelmed every last shred of composure. His body had betrayed him in its desperation to stay alive.

Still, he didn't scream.

He couldn't.

His voice was trapped behind a wall of ice lodged in his throat. Every cell in his body told him to run, but his legs were anchored in the tent floor. He clutched the flashlight tighter, as if the narrow beam of light could somehow shield them from what stood just inches away.

And then, just as suddenly as it had appeared, the creature lurched backward. Its sinewy frame gave a violent shudder. One long, clawed hand twitched once, twice—and then dropped to its side. With a low, guttural groan, it turned and melted back into the darkness beyond the firelight, its grotesque silhouette swallowed by the woods.

Jason remained frozen, staring into the trees long after the creature had vanished.

Greg, ever the skeptic, initially attempted to rationalize the situation. "Probably just a bear or some wild animal," he muttered, though his voice lacked conviction. His eyes darted nervously, betraying his attempt to maintain composure.

Megan, who had been closest to Jason and Sierra's tent, was visibly shaken. Her face drained of color as she recounted the events. "I heard the scream... it was like nothing I've ever heard before. And the tent... it was shredded, like something had torn through it.

Liam, the group's self-appointed leader, tried to maintain order. "We need to stay calm," he urged, though his clenched fists and rapid breathing betrayed his own fear. "Let's gather our things and head to the ranger station. We'll figure this out together.

Rachel, who had been sitting by the campfire when the scream pierced the night, was in a state of disbelief. "This can't be happening," she whispered repeatedly, as if saying it aloud would make it untrue. "We were just telling stories, and now... this?

Tom, the most level-headed of the group, took charge. "Everyone, stay close. We're not splitting up. Let's check on the others and then head out. No one goes anywhere alone."

Tom's voice was steady, but there was a tremor beneath it. "No one goes anywhere alone," he repeated, his eyes scanning the darkness beyond the firelight. "We wait here until the sheriff arrives."

No one argued. The remaining campers huddled together around the dying embers of the fire, their once-carefree night now warped into something unreal. Sierra still hadn't come to. Jason cradled her gently beside what was left of their tent, murmuring her name and checking her breathing. His face was pale, and a dark stain spread across the front of his jeans — not from injury, but from fear.

I ran to the trailhead," Megan said, breathless. "There's a pay phone there. I called the operator, told her it was an emergency. I didn't know what to say. I think I just blurted out that something attacked us. An animal, maybe. I don't know. But they're sending someone. They said they'd send help. "What kind of animal rips open a tent like that and just vanishes?" Greg muttered. "And that scream... that wasn't no animal. That was..."

Nobody finished the sentence.

They sat in stunned silence, the only sounds the crackling of cooling logs and the occasional pop of sap in the firewood. In the distance, the woods creaked and shifted in the wind. Every snap of a twig, every rustle of leaves sent pulses of fear through the group.

Rachel was staring at the trees, eyes wide. "Do you guys feel like it's... still out there? Watching us?"

No one responded, but several heads turned toward the darkened tree line.

Liam stood, rubbing his arms for warmth or comfort. "We should stoke the fire. Keep it bright. Whatever that thing was, it didn't like the flashlight."

Tom nodded and grabbed some firewood from the nearby stack, throwing logs onto the glowing coals.

Sparks spiraled up, briefly illuminating their anxious faces.

For the next fifteen minutes, they waited, no one speaking, barely breathing. Sierra stirred finally, groaning softly. Jason's eyes filled with tears as he helped her sit up.

Then came the distant rumble of tires on gravel. Headlights cut through the trees. Relief flooded the group like a wave as the flashing red and blue lights of a county cruiser followed, bouncing over the potholes leading to their campsite.

The sheriff's truck rolled to a stop beside the circle of tents. Two deputies and a paramedic climbed out, their eyes sweeping the scene.

Jason stood, his voice hoarse. "She fainted. And, someone attacked us. Something…"

The sheriff, a heavyset man in his fifties named Dalton Griggs, stepped forward with the slow calm of someone who had seen too much and still not enough.

"Slow down, son," he said. "We'll get to the bottom of this. Let's start with who's hurt."

As the paramedic checked Sierra's vitals, the sheriff moved to inspect the shredded tent. His eyes narrowed, jaw tightening as he ran a hand along the slashed fabric.

He looked back at the group.

"What the hell kind of bear does *this*?" he muttered under his breath.

Chapter 20: The Whispering Pines

The incident at Pine Hollow Campground hit the local papers within a day. The sheriff's official statement downplayed the details, citing "wildlife disturbance and possible alcohol-fueled panic." But within hours, the real story had already begun to ripple through the community in the way stories always did up north—by voice, by campfire, and over cracked mugs at the diner counter.

The tent had been torn nearly in half. Sierra was unconscious when first responders arrived, still trembling even after waking. Jason was pale, barely able to speak, his voice dry and cracked as he relayed what he saw. The other campers corroborated the strange sounds, the guttural screams, and the long moaning that had haunted the lake's edge for weeks.

At first, people wanted to dismiss it. The Northwoods had always had its legends, tales of hermits, shadowy shapes in the trees, and eerie cries from the deep forest. But this was different. There was a name now. A face, even if only described in shaken fragments.

Schiefe.

The name alone was enough to make some old-timers raise their brows and mutter under their breath. "You mean Corby Schieffen?" they'd ask quietly, incredulously. "The bait shop kid?"

But it wasn't long before disbelief gave way to fascination. Then fear.

The wreckage at the campground gave the tale weight. Campers packed up early, canceling weekend reservations and heading home. Locals who'd once laughed at the idea of a wandering figure stalking the woods now refused to walk their dogs after dark. Some stopped fishing altogether, saying the lake had gone "wrong." There was something in the water, they whispered. And something watching from the trees.

A figure crossing old logging roads at dusk. Hunched, fast-moving. Too big to be a man, too upright to be a bear. One woman said it paused by her mailbox and stared at the house for almost ten minutes, then disappeared just as her husband pulled into the drive.

Another man, a retired mill worker, heard knocking on his back window after midnight. Slow, rhythmic taps. When he turned on the porch light, no one was there. But in the dewy grass were prints, bare human feet, large, uneven, and smeared with something dark.

They called it paranoia. Cabin fever. Superstition. But fear is a wildfire in small towns. And this one spread fast.

The diner that once buzzed with morning chatter turned tense and quiet. Hunters kept rifles propped by their doors. Parents walked their kids to school even though the bus still ran. The whispers became theories, the theories became truths. And everywhere you went—from the post office to the boat launch—people spoke his name in lowered tones:

"Schiefe."

Some said it wasn't Corby at all. That it was something born of him. A thing made from chemicals and rage. Others said it was Corby, twisted by his own creation, his body fused with lakewater and poison and failure. A ghost with skin.

And in Stillwater, where he had once grown up as just a quiet, curious boy with a love of science and fish, the bait shop stood as a blackened reminder. Charred boards, broken glass, the stove melted and collapsed in on itself. Locals gave it a wide berth. Some wanted it torn down. Others said to leave it, the lake needed a place to bury its secrets.

And that night, like so many before, those near the shoreline reported hearing it again.

The shrill, inhuman cry that echoed across the black water. Long, mournful, and full of something older than pain. The name that curled like a blade in the mist.

"Scheeeeeiiiiiiieeeeeefffff…"

The Northwoods held its breath.

And the pines whispered stories only the dark could understand.

Chapter 21: Full Moon in the Pines

The moon hung fat and full above the Northwoods, bloated and glowing like a pale eye, its cold light bleeding through the towering crowns of pine trees. The shadows it cast were long and skeletal, stretching across the cracked, winding driveway like black veins. The night air was sharp and still, cold enough to bite the lungs. Everything smelled of damp earth and pine needles and old, wet bark.

Somewhere deeper in the forest, a great horned owl called, low and distant. The sound didn't echo. It just hung there, suspended in the freezing dark like a warning.

At the far end of the winding drive, half-buried in a shallow hill overgrown with brambles and frost-cloaked thickets, the Red Antler Supper Club gave off a golden glow. Its windows were frosted with breath and condensation, foggy from the warmth within, but the light still spilled faintly onto the ground, cutting a fragile line against the tide of dark pressing in around it. The building looked like it had grown there rather than been built, hunched low with a sagging roof and smoke curling thinly from the chimney.

The woods crowded close. The trees didn't sway. They just stood…listening.

Inside, the Red Antler was alive, in that muted way northern bars are in the off-season. Low voices murmured, forks clicked, glasses clinked, and the occasional burst of laughter sparked and fizzled out like a match held too long. Not many people, but enough to fill the space. Enough to pretend things were normal.

Wood-paneled walls darkened by years of smoke and polish held up shelves cluttered with stuffed trout, antlers, and framed Polaroids of long-dead men holding larger-than-life fish. The bar glowed with soft amber, the ice machine clicked intermittently, and an electric candle flickered at each booth.

In the corner, under the gaze of a dust-worn buck head and sagging strings of yellow fairy bulbs, sat Chives. His cranberry tuxedo shimmered faintly in the low light, a pop of theatricality against the backdrop of browns and shadows. He leaned into the piano, fingers moving with flourished elegance across the black-and-white keys. It was the kind of performance born from hundreds of nights just like this: small towns, small rooms, the same five songs, played with a confidence so smooth it looked careless.

He smiled at the woman who laughed too loudly at her husband's joke. He nodded warmly to a man raising a glass in his direction. He played *Mancini*, then slid into *Gershwin*, blending the old standards with a touch of blues, a splash of something smoky and loose. His smile was practiced. Polished. The kind people trusted. But it never quite made it to his eyes.

Chives was a man who wore charm like cologne—thick and unavoidable. Even here, even now, his gaze lingered a beat too long on waitresses. His tongue flicked to the corner of his mouth when he smiled at younger patrons. Just enough to unsettle if you were paying attention. But no one was.

They were warm. Safe. Inside.

Out there, the woods breathed.

The night outside the Red Antler was absolute.

From the far edge of the parking lot, where the yellow floodlight couldn't quite reach, something moved. Slow. Deliberate.

A shape emerged from the tree line, a tall silhouette hunched unnaturally forward, limbs swaying like branches, slow and dragging. It stayed just inside the dark, the way animals do when they don't want to be seen but don't care if you sense them. The thing breathed heavily, the cold pulling vapor from its lungs in thick, curling ribbons.

It stepped closer.

Its gait was wrong. Lurching, off-balance. Each footfall sank with weight and purpose. Its shoulders were broad, neck barely there, and its arms were long, too long, reaching past the knees. The hands that swayed at its sides ended not in fingers, but in *two* long, malformed appendages, mutated index and middle fingers tipped with curved, razor-like claws. Like hooked knives. They scraped against each other as it walked.

Scrrritch... scritch... scritch...

The sound was dry, metallic. Almost surgical. Like a butcher dragging steel across steel in the dark.

The figure pressed forward through the frozen brush and stopped just outside one of the glowing windows. Low to the ground now, crouched like a stalking animal. Steam rose off his back, catching the light. His hair was matted and wild, his jaw half-hinged, breath leaking in rasps that sounded half-mutter, half-choke.

Schief.

No one called him that anymore. Maybe no one ever really had. But that was what he was. A name boiled down from fear, from whispered stories and burned-out memories.

He leaned in close to the glass, and in the haze of condensation, he peered inside.

The room was warm and full of flickering yellow light. People clinked glasses, bit into battered fish, wiped ketchup from their chins. Oblivious.

Schief scanned the room slowly. His breath misted the window in wet fog, and he blinked once, slow and deliberate, his eyes murky and sunken, but not blind.

Then he saw him.

Chives.

The man was finishing a light-hearted tune, turning on the bench to speak to someone at the bar, smiling like a salesman, like he was always closing some quiet deal. He leaned toward a woman in a tight sweater, gave her a look—teeth just a little too bared, pupils just a little too wide. It was subtle, but it stuck out.

Schief froze.

That smile—too long, too close, too used to being tolerated. Something in Schief twitched. A low groan caught in his throat. His breath quickened, clouding the window.

Then, from inside, a voice carried.

A man clapped Chives on the shoulder as he passed and said, with good cheer: "Legendary stuff tonight, *Chives*. You're killin' it, man."

And that was it.

The name. Spoken cleanly, casually. Like it didn't mean anything.

But Schief heard it.

And he repeated it.

Low at first. Just a hiss in the back of his throat, barely shaped by the warped muscles of his mouth.

"Schhiiives…"

The clawed fingers rubbed together again, metal-on-metal.

"Ssscchhhhiivvves…"

121

Drool pooled at the edge of his bottom lip. His tongue twitched against broken teeth. The veins in his neck began to bulge. A low gurgling sound built up from his chest like something drowning.

"Schiieves...   gghhhharrghhh... ssccchiieeevess..."

His whole body tensed, vibrating with an unfamiliar, primal need. The kind that came before fire. Before tools. Before words.

Inside, Chives played on, completely unaware.

Outside, Schief lowered himself further into the darkness, his fingers twitching in slow arcs across the bark of the window frame. The claws **scraped**, leaving deep parallel marks. Not hard. Not angry. Almost lovingly.

He pressed his forehead against the fogged glass.

"Sssschhiieeevess..."

The last song of the night was *Moon River*, played slow and warm, Chives letting the final note hang just long enough to feel elegant. He gave a slight bow, a tired flourish, and stepped down from the piano bench. A few lingering patrons offered lazy applause. Someone shouted a thanks. Someone else tossed a tip.

He smiled through it all. That too-long smile. The same one he gave everyone, as if every interaction were part of some performance he'd never been asked to give. Then he gathered his sheet music, tucked it into a cracked leather folder, and slipped his arms into his coat.

The moment he opened the back door and stepped into the night, the warmth of the supper club vanished behind him like a held breath.

The cold hit his face like a slap. He stood there a second too long, adjusting his collar, waiting for his eyes to adjust to the murk. The parking lot was still and empty. Gravel crunched beneath his shoes as he stepped forward.

The *Red Antler* let out a last breath of warm air before the door swung closed behind him with a quiet thump. After that, nothing.

No sound.

Just his own footsteps.

And his own breath.

Chives pulled his keys from his coat pocket, the metal jingling softly in the stillness. He moved toward his faded red Toyota hatchback, which sat crooked near the edge of the lot, the rear bumper tilted slightly from an old fender bender.

His boots slipped a little in a patch of frost.

He laughed, one short, nervous bark. "Careful now," he muttered to himself, a habit he picked up after too many years alone in motel lounges and gas station bathrooms.

Then the keys slipped from his hand.

They clattered to the gravel with a metallic clink that sounded *too loud* in the silence.

He crouched to pick them up, his knees popping as he did. That was when he heard it.

A sound, *barely* there.

A whisper of metal.

Scritch... scritch... scritch...

It came from the treeline behind him, maybe thirty feet back, where the floodlight barely touched.

Chives froze. Not because he understood what he was hearing, but because something primitive inside him did.

His fingers closed around the keys. Slowly, he stood and turned toward the woods.

Nothing.

Just trees. A lot of trees. A windless dark.

He squinted into the shadows, heart starting to thump harder in his chest.

"Denny?" he said, voice cracking just a little. "That you? This ain't funny, man."

Silence.

He turned back to the car.

Then the sound came again, closer this time. Same rhythm. **Scritch... scritch...**

Like knives whispering against each other.

And then—

"Sssschhhiiieeves..."

The voice came from somewhere too close.

It wasn't shouted. It wasn't clear. It was like someone trying to force the name through a throat full of broken glass.

Chives spun.

There he was.

A shape, just outside the light.

Tall. Crooked. Slow.

The creature stepped forward, and Chives finally *saw* him. The arms, the elongated hands. The **two fingers**, each too long, each ending in claws that glinted in the moonlight like polished bone. His mouth hung open, lips split and wet, breath whistling through a twisted tongue.

"SSSCHIIIEEEEVES—"

The scream tore through the trees like a knife. It wasn't loud—it was *wrong*. Piercing. Sick. A sound that felt like it could splinter bone.

Chives ran.

Not to the door. Not to the club.

He bolted toward the woods.

He didn't even think. There was no plan. No logic. Just **fear**.

The woods closed around him like a mouth.

Branches snapped against Chives's coat. Brambles clawed at his pants, tearing fabric, drawing thin red lines down his shins. Cold mud oozed from nowhere, swallowing his feet as he stumbled deeper into the trees. The shadows between the pines flickered with moonlight. Nothing made sense.

Behind him—close—came the sound again.

Scritch... scritch... scritch...

Not footsteps.

Fingernails.

Those two long claws dragging together in a slow, deliberate rhythm, sharpening themselves. Preparing.

"Sssschhiieeevessss…"

The voice oozed through the trees like smoke.

Chives crashed through a tangle of saplings, one branch whipping him hard across the cheek. He tripped and fell, smacked the frozen ground with a thud, and scrambled back up, his hands trembling so badly he could barely keep his footing. Leaves stuck to the blood on his face. His breath came in wet, choking gasps.

The forest was no longer passive. It felt **alive**, hostile. Every root rose up to catch his foot, every vine reached to snag his sleeve. Brambles lashed at his thighs like they wanted him down. The very air felt thick, syrupy with rot and cold.

He whimpered. Actually whimpered. A pathetic, primal sound that came from somewhere deep in his chest.

Then that other sound again—

Scritch. Scritch. Scritch.

Sssscchhiiiiiiiiiiiiiiivesssss

It wasn't random anymore. It had a cadence. A purpose.

Chives turned, wild-eyed, scanning the dark. His legs were covered in mud and blood now, one shoe lost somewhere behind. His socks were soaked. His teeth chattered, not from cold, but from raw, unfiltered dread.

"God—please—" he rasped, stumbling over a log. "Who are you? What the f*** are you—?!"

From behind, impossibly close now, the answer came:

"Ssscccchhiiieeevvves…"

The trees swayed, even though there was no wind.

Chives turned and ran again, this time blind, crashing forward. He couldn't tell where the supper club was anymore. Couldn't tell where he'd come from. The moonlight kept shifting, no longer above him but between the trees, as if the forest itself wanted to confuse him.

He slipped again, this time falling hard. His ankle twisted with a sick pop. He cried out—loud, desperate.

That's when he heard the breathing.

Heavy. Wet. Close.

Behind him, something stepped lightly over the underbrush—so close he could hear the crunch of leaves. Then came the scrape of claw on bark. Not a chase. Not frantic.

Just **following**. Watching.

A whisper of movement passed within feet of him, just out of sight.

Chives held his breath, eyes wild, mouth open in a silent scream.

Then—

Nothing.

No breathing.

No scraping.

Just the silence of the forest, heavy and endless.

He blinked. Tried to sit up. His fingers sank into something cold and spongy. Moss? Mud? He didn't know.

He turned slowly.

And he saw—

Nothing.

Just trees.

But his eyes widened. His mouth opened.

And he screamed.

Only for a moment.

The scream was short, choked, smothered by something unseen.

And then the forest went still again.

Somewhere above, a crow lifted from a branch and vanished into the dark.

Snow began to fall—soft and soundless.

It settled gently across the brambles and mud, across broken branches and torn roots.

And not far from where the scream had died, **a small splash of crimson** bloomed across the fresh white, staining it like a secret the woods had no intention of telling.

The trees whispered nothing.

The woods held what they had taken.

Chapter 22: What the Pines Remember

The sun rose pale and indifferent over the Northwoods, casting its washed-out light through the brittle arms of the pines. The frost glistened on everything, rooftops, gravel, branches, like the woods had been sealed in glass. No birds sang. No wind stirred. The air was still.

Too still.

The long dirt driveway to the Red Antler Supper Club lay quiet, rutted and frozen. Tire tracks crisscrossed the gravel, some recent, some faded into frost. The world looked paused, as if the forest itself was holding something back.

Jasper pulled his truck into the parking lot just before seven. The crunch beneath his tires was too loud, breaking the silence like a cracked bone. He turned the engine off but didn't move right away. He just sat there, gloved hands resting on the steering wheel, staring out at the weather-worn building.

The supper club looked different in daylight, hollowed out, colder, smaller somehow. The warm yellow windows from last night were now dulled panes of condensation and grime. A half-frozen smear of something brownish-red streaked the glass beside the front door. Probably spilled sauce. Probably.

He squinted at the corner of the lot. There, slumped just past the broken floodlight, was Chives's old red Toyota.

It was parked crooked, angled slightly downhill, like it had rolled and never been corrected. The driver's side door was cracked open. Not wide. Just enough to matter. Just enough to feel wrong.

Jasper felt it in his gut before his brain caught up.

Something had happened.

He opened the door and stepped out into the cold. The gravel crunched beneath his boots, sharp and uneven. His breath came out in plumes. The air smelled faintly of pine sap, exhaust, and something else, something sour, metallic, hard to name.

"Chives?" he called, softly, like saying it too loud might bring something toward him.

Nothing.

He walked slowly across the lot, eyes flicking to the tree line. The woods loomed just behind the building, close and dark, the way they always were. But this morning, they felt closer. Like they'd crept forward in the night. Like they were listening.

As he approached the Toyota, he noticed the frost melted away along the driver's side door. A wide smear, hand-shaped, had dragged across the frame and left behind a greasy arc.

Below it, scattered in the gravel, were keys. Chives's, unmistakably, cluttered with mismatched tags, a cracked ivory piano key keychain, and a green bottle opener shaped like a trout. They were splayed as if they'd been dropped mid-run.

Jasper crouched to pick them up, fingers numbing fast in the air. The keys were half-frozen into the grit, and when he pulled them free, a soft crackle of ice broke off the keyring.

He straightened, scanning the car's interior. His gloves were in the passenger seat, palms up. The dome light was dead.

Jasper's heart knocked against his ribs.

He turned to the woods again.

There was no movement. No wind. No animal chatter. The whole world felt vacuum-sealed.

Jasper retreated to the supper club and nervously dialed for the sheriff.

Something was gone. And something else was still out there.

The sheriff's cruiser appeared first, headlights slicing through the lingering fog like twin beacons in a world of gray and shadow. The engine's steady rumble softened to a low growl as the car eased to a stop on the frost-cracked gravel of the Red Antler parking lot. Moments later, another patrol vehicle pulled in behind it, the tires crunching sharply on the frozen earth, followed by a steady stream of deputies emerging from their cars, bundled against the biting cold. Their breath drifted in white clouds that seemed to hang in the air long after they vanished.

Jasper stepped forward, his voice tight with a mix of urgency and disbelief. "It's Chives. His car's here, door's open, keys scattered on the ground. But… he's gone. No sign of him anywhere."

The sheriff was a broad-shouldered man, weathered by years of cold seasons and harder realities. His eyes narrowed beneath a heavy brow, scanning the parking lot, the edge of the woods, the cracked driveway. "Alright," he said, voice low but firm. "We don't waste time. We'll spread out, call his name. Move carefully, this forest holds its secrets well."

Without ceremony, the deputies dispersed, slipping like shadows into the thick stands of pines. Their boots pressed down on brittle needles and frozen earth, the only sounds their careful steps and low calls—"Chives! Hey, Chives!"—echoing softly against the vast, silent backdrop of the woods.

Jasper stood by the car, every sense straining. The cold seemed sharper now, more biting, as if the forest itself exhaled a chill meant to warn him away. The scent of pine resin mingled with damp earth and something darker, something faintly metallic that set his teeth on edge. His throat tightened, a dry knot of worry settling deep.

Branches creaked overhead, and distant, disjointed animal calls punctuated the heavy silence.

But beneath it all, Jasper felt the forest's quiet pulse—a slow, ancient rhythm that thrummed beneath the bark and moss.

Hours crawled by with agonizing slowness. The calls grew hoarse, the searchers' voices thinning and losing hope. Then the tracking dogs arrived, lean, eager, noses pressed to the ground. They darted forward, weaving through the tangled underbrush with relentless focus, tails stiff as they followed a scent trail only they could perceive.

The dogs' sudden halt near a ring of gnarled old pines sent a ripple of unease through the search party. They pawed at the frozen dirt and stared up at the bark, revealing deep, narrow gouges carved into the wood—too straight, too deliberate to be the work of bears or random damage. The cuts ran vertical, like the scratch marks of claws but unnaturally precise.

The sheriff knelt, brushing frost from one of the scars, his eyes shadowed. "These marks… someone, or something, wanted to leave a message."

Jasper swallowed hard. The forest seemed to lean in closer, the branches whispering secrets just out of reach. Stories stirred at the edges of his mind—the old warnings about the woods, the vanished man, the shape lurking just beyond the tree line.

This was no accident. No stray animal.

This was something else.

Something older.

Something waiting.

The search party's calls had slowly faded into near silence, swallowed by the dense forest pressing in on all sides. Jasper's boots crunched over brittle needles and frozen earth, his breath rising in ragged clouds in the cold morning air. The pine trunks stood like ancient sentinels, their needles whispering secrets on a faint breeze. The weak morning sun filtered through the branches, casting fractured patterns of light and shadow over the tangled forest floor.

Deputy Carlisle moved ahead cautiously, eyes scanning the uneven ground where roots twisted like old bones, and thorn bushes snagged at anything passing through. Then, suddenly, he stopped, his gaze fixed on something barely visible beneath the forest litter.

Jasper hurried forward, his heart tightening as he saw what Carlisle had found.

There, curled against the base of a towering pine, lay Chives.

His body was folded tightly in a fetal position, clothes shredded and dirty. Pale, bruised skin showed beneath ragged fabric. His arms and legs bore superficial scratches from brambles. His back had much deeper lacerations that still oozed blood into the thirsty forest floor. His back looked like he had been whipped but the lashings were much deeper. Some of the openings revealed his ribs. His hair was matted, face pale and drawn, lips cracked and moving with shallow, uneven breaths as he quietly uttered something. The fingers on both of his has were mangled, as if caught in some type of heavy farming machinery. Fingers pointing in several directions, the bones in his hands obvious shattered but by what?

A hush fell over the group. Even the wind seemed to hold its breath.

Carlisle knelt and gently turned Chives's head. His eyes wide, glassy, unfocused. His gaze seemed locked beyond the trees, distant and haunted.

A faint, rasping whisper escaped his lips:

"Schiiieves…"

The name hung in the cold air, heavy with something unspoken.

Jasper swallowed hard, a chill crawling down his spine. The forest's stillness was suffocating, as if it were watching, waiting. Behind Chives, deep, narrow marks scored the bark of the pine, too clean and straight to be animal scratches.

No one spoke. The weight of the moment pressed down like a silent storm.

They moved carefully, lifting Chives onto a stretcher. His body was limp but trembling, fragile. The medics worked swiftly but gently, their faces pale and serious. Jasper saw the tight set of their jaws, the quiet concern behind their professionalism.

As they carried him through the woods, the trees seemed to close in, shadows deepening around them. The search party followed in silence, each step a reminder that the forest had given up only part of its secret, and still held the rest close.

The cold sun climbed higher, but the forest remained dark at its core. The questions left behind cut sharp and cold.

The ambulance tore through the pale dawn, siren wailing into the cold Northwoods morning. Inside, the world was reduced to harsh, shifting shadows and the faint stench of antiseptic. Chives lay strapped to the stretcher, his body unnervingly still except for the shallow, uneven rise and fall of his chest. His eyes were open, wide, glassy, and vacant, staring unblinkingly into some dark distance no one else could see.

His skin was clammy, slick with cold sweat that traced erratic rivulets down his face and neck. The faint, ragged breaths escaped his cracked lips in irregular gasps, as if his lungs were fighting to pull air through a haze of panic and despair. Every now and then, he'd murmur a single word—broken, guttural, barely audible: "Schiiieves…"

The paramedics worked around him with practiced efficiency, checking vitals, securing IV lines, but their glances flicked to each other, betraying unease.

On the ambulance's rough ride to St. Agnes Hospital, every bump and swerve seemed to rattle what little composure he had left. His mangled fingers twitched uncontrollably, as if grappling with unseen chains. The once-confident fingers that danced across piano keys now trembled like brittle leaves in a storm.

At the hospital, doctors stitched his wounds and set his fractures. But their instruments could do nothing for the deeper fractures, the ones that had shattered his mind.

Psychiatrists spoke in cold, clinical terms: "Acute psychological trauma," "dissociation," "catatonic state." Terms that barely scraped the surface of what they were facing.

Chives lay silent, unresponsive. His body was gaunt, hollowed out by fear and exhaustion. He refused to speak or eat, his lips parting only to repeat that broken mantra—a desperate chant that twisted in his throat: "Schiiieves... Schiiieves..."

Nurses whispered about the strange way he avoided sound—flinching at footsteps, recoiling from voices, trembling at the slightest touch. Music, once his refuge, now made him convulse with panic. The radio was silenced; the usual hospital sounds dampened in a futile attempt to soothe his fraying nerves.

Days bled into nights. The man who had once owned the supper club's stage was a ghost trapped inside his own mind, drifting further from reality.

At Glenwood Care Center, far from the warmth of the supper club, Chives became a haunting shadow by the window, his eyes fixed blankly on the dark forest beyond, yet seeing nothing but the void inside his own fractured mind.

He sat wrapped in a thin hospital blanket, hands twitching violently, lips murmuring that cursed name over and over, the syllables cracked and ragged like fractured glass: "Schiiieves… Schiiieves…"

Sometimes, a brittle, broken laugh would escape—a sound void of joy, hollow and chilling. Then tears would follow, shaking his frail frame as though the darkness clawed at his soul from within.

Visitors tried to reach him, but his gaze cut through them like ice. The man they once knew—the charming, confident pianist—was gone. In his place was a broken vessel, a living testament to an unspeakable horror.

Jasper watched helplessly, frustration and despair knitting his brow. The man he had found in the woods was now trapped in a prison no one else could see—a terror far worse than any physical wound.

And through it all, the one word never left Chives's trembling lips.

"Schiiieves…"

The true nightmare was not what the woods had done to him. It was what remained afterward—the shattered mind, the haunting silence, and the endless echo of a name whispered like a curse in the dark.

Jasper sat just outside Chives's room, the sterile glow of the hallway lights casting long shadows against the pale linoleum floor. He clenched his fists, fingers digging into his knees as he stared at the closed door. Behind it, the man he'd found in the woods was slipping further away, not just physically, but from everything that made him who he was.

The nurses warned him to be patient, to give Chives time. But patience was a thin thread stretched taut over an abyss. Every day, Jasper felt it fray a little more.

The muffled sounds that slipped through the door, the whispering hums, the soft sobs, the sudden sharp bursts of incoherent laughter, were like echoes from some place Jasper couldn't follow. Each time the name "Schiiieves" broke through the silence, a chill ran down his spine, cold and relentless.

The room itself seemed swallowed in silence, except for the faintest hum of the machines keeping Chives alive. The air smelled faintly of antiseptic and something else, something stale, like the residue of forgotten nightmares.

Jasper's mind raced, filled with memories of the night he found Chives. The scattered keys on the frozen ground. The way his eyes had seemed both vacant and filled with terror all at once. He thought about the claw marks on the tree bark, the unanswered questions, and the way the forest had seemed to close in around them both.

He wanted to believe that somewhere deep inside, the man who'd made the piano sing still existed. But the silence suggested otherwise.

At night, Jasper dreamt of the woods. Of twisted branches reaching like claws, of whispers carried on the wind calling out that name—Schiiieves. He woke gasping, heart pounding, fingers trembling as if he'd felt the brush of those long, cruel nails.

He hated the helplessness, the way the horror had crept from the shadows into their lives, leaving nothing but a broken shell behind.

And yet, even in the sterile quiet of the care center, Jasper knew the woods weren't done with them. Not yet.

As Jasper walked down the long, sterile hallway toward the exit, the fractured sounds behind him twisted through the silence—maniacal laughter laced with ragged sobs and desperate, incoherent murmurs. The haunting cacophony echoed off the pale walls, growing faint as he put distance between himself and the room. His skin prickled, every nerve on edge, and though his heart ached with care for Chives, he knew deep down he could never return here, not to this place where the light felt so cold and the shadows so alive.

Chapter 23: Lover's Lane

The Northwoods breathed under the light of a swollen, silvery full moon. Pines stretched tall, their jagged silhouettes scratching at the night sky like broken claws. Shadows pooled in hollows and pressed into the earth like bruises, thick between the brambles that twisted across the forest floor like the gnarled fingers of something ancient and long-buried.

The air smelled of pine sap and damp soil, but something else rode beneath it—cold and metallic, like rusted iron. A stillness hung in the trees that didn't feel natural. The kind of silence that suggested something was waiting.

A narrow dirt road cut through the underbrush, forgotten by time and mostly erased by nature. There, half-sunk in soft mud, sat a battered 1965 Chevrolet Nova, its steel body dulled by rust, its taillights like two dying embers in the dark.

Inside, warmth pulsed from the old vents, and the haze of breath and body heat clung to the windows. A classic rock song played low on the radio, muffled and warbling through old speakers. It should have been romantic, but something about the way the sound was swallowed by the night made it feel off. Like the woods were listening.

Kyle reached across the driver's seat, hand brushing Misty's wrist. His grin was half-assured, half-nervous, like a guy trying not to admit the woods had gotten to him.

"You cold?" he asked.

Misty sat tense, jacket pulled tight around her neck, her breath visible in short, quick bursts. "A little," she said, eyes flicking toward the window. "It's weird out here."

Kyle smirked, sliding his hand across her shoulder. "Weird's good. Nobody around. No one watching. Just us and the stars."

Misty didn't smile. Her fingers toyed with the zipper of her jacket. "Yeah, but... it's quiet. Too quiet."

Kyle chuckled, but his laugh was thin. "Come on. It's the woods. That's how they work. Trees, dirt, some squirrels doing freaky squirrel things. Nature stuff." Misty didn't answer. Her eyes had locked on something deeper in the forest. "It just feels... off. Like the trees are breathing."

Kyle followed her gaze but saw only darkness and the flicker of moonlight through the branches.

"You've been watching too many horror movies," he said, brushing her hair behind her ear.

She pulled away gently. "Did you hear that?"

Kyle turned the volume knob down.

Silence.

The kind of silence that rings in the ears.

Then—**a faint rustle**.

Not the wind. Not leaves.

A drag.

A slow shuffle through dirt and fallen pine needles.

"Probably a raccoon," Kyle muttered, his tone less sure now.

Misty hugged her arms tighter. "That didn't sound like a raccoon."

He reached out, found her hand. "Look, we're fine. We're in the car. Doors locked. Full tank. Just a little spring chill and your imagination."

A **soft thud** landed against the rear passenger door. Misty flinched.

Kyle twisted around. "Okay, now that... that was something."

They both sat frozen. Misty slowly turned her head toward the rear window, but it was fogged, the outside obscured by a thick haze of condensation. She reached forward and wiped at the glass with her sleeve.

Nothing. Just trees and night.

Then, softly—

scrape...

A sharp, deliberate drag of something hard—*metal or bone*—along the side of the car. It started at the trunk and moved toward the back door. Long and slow.

Screeeeee...

The sound wasn't loud. It wasn't meant to be. It was intimate. Close.

Misty whispered, "Kyle, do something."

He turned the key halfway, the dashboard flickering to life. The engine didn't turn over yet—just the lights and the hum of circuits coming alive.

And then came the voice.

A low, **hissing rasp**, like steam escaping a broken pipe. A ruined voice.

"Sssschhhhhhieeefff..."

Both of them froze.

The name hissed again, slower this time, garbled and moist:

"Mmmmissssschy... Schief..."

The sound didn't seem to come from outside the car, not exactly. It was like it came from the trees themselves—or closer. Maybe just inches away.

Kyle turned the key fully.

Click. Click. Roar.

The Nova's engine jumped to life.

But Misty wasn't looking at the wheel.

She was looking at the side window.

Because something was pressed against it now.

A face.

A **face** pressed against the fogged glass— misshapen, sagging, and blistered like wax run under flame. Its skin was warped and unnatural, stretched in places, melted in others. Scars puckered down its cheeks, one side fused tight as if burned and never healed. The lips, if they could be called that, were split and twisted into a snarling grimace. **Jagged teeth,** blackened and broken, gleamed through thick ropes of saliva that slithered down the glass.

And the eyes.

One was sealed shut by melted flesh, but the other, wide, bloodshot, and too wet—locked onto Misty with animal hatred.

Her breath caught in her throat. She couldn't scream.

Then it hissed again, its deformed mouth struggling to shape the sounds:

"Sssschhhiieefff... Mmmissschyyy..."

Misty's scream exploded from her chest as the **window shattered**, glass bursting inward in a violent crack. A **long, thin arm** reached through the broken opening, impossibly long, its skin raw and sagging, stretched over bone like leather. At the end of it, **only two fingers** protruded, **the index and middle**, each grotesquely extended into long, tapering claws, curling slightly at the ends like ancient hooks.

They slashed downward.

Kyle cried out as the claws raked across his shoulder, shredding his jacket and leaving a burning line of blood. Misty turned to scramble over the center console, but Schief's second swipe caught her upper arm. The talon tore through her jacket, slicing skin, heat and pain flaring through her.

She fell back, gasping. Her blood smeared across the dashboard in a red streak.

147

Kyle slammed the car into drive.

The Nova lurched forward, tires spinning in the dirt before catching traction.

"HOLD ON!" he yelled.

Behind them, a scream tore loose from the forest, not human, not animal. Something **feral**, something birthed in **pain and rage**.

"SCHEEEEEIIIIIF!"

The car roared down the narrow path, gravel clattering against the undercarriage. The trees closed in on either side, and the Nova's headlights danced wildly over roots and ruts.

Misty twisted in her seat, pressing her bloodied arm against the door for support. "He's still there—he's still coming!"

Kyle risked a glance into the rearview mirror.

Schief was running.

Not just running—**keeping up**. His body flailed forward with unnatural speed, each step more like a *lunge* than a stride. His arms hung too low, fingers trailing the dirt. His claws caught against rocks and roots, sparking and slicing, his ragged body illuminated briefly by moonlight and taillights.

"Jesus—" Kyle muttered. "That's not—he can't—"

He punched the gas. The car surged to forty, then fifty, but the dirt road twisted, winding hard to the left.

The tires skidded, the whole vehicle drifting sideways for a heartbeat before correcting.

Schief didn't slow. He darted into the brush beside the road, crashing through branches, arms snapping limbs away like paper.

The radio still played, crackling beneath the screams and roar of the engine—a faint, distorted track now looping a line unintelligibly, as if the car itself was losing its grip on sanity.

Misty clutched her wound, sobbing. "He's faster than us—he's not human, Kyle!"

"I KNOW!" Kyle shouted, breath ragged. His hands gripped the wheel so tight his knuckles gleamed white. "We just need pavement—this road's slowing us down!"

The Nova bounced violently, the undercarriage scraping stone.

Behind them, the forest came alive with crashing sounds, branches snapping, leaves scattering. Schief screamed again:

"SCHEEEEIIIIIF!"

Then—

THUMP.

The entire car jerked. Misty screamed again.

Schief's claws had caught the rear bumper.

Kyle floored it.

The car bucked and fishtailed, stones erupting in a spray behind the tires. The sound of metal being torn reached their ears—a grinding shriek—and then a wet slap as something hit the trunk.

Misty looked back, eyes wide with terror.

Schief had **climbed onto the back of the car**.

His face appeared again in the shattered rear window—closer now, illuminated red by the brake lights. His mouth moved, whispering as drool slid across the broken glass.

"Schiiieeff... Misschyyy…"

His clawed hand slammed down again—**GUNK**—denting the trunk, carving two **deep vertical gouges** into the steel.

Kyle swerved.

The road turned to gravel, then dirt again. The curve ahead sloped upward toward the old county highway.

Kyle shouted, "If we hit the blacktop, we might throw him!"

"GO!" Misty screamed.

Kyle slammed the car into drive, tires spinning on the dirt before they caught. The Nova roared forward, bumping along the uneven trail as branches whipped past the windows.

Behind them, from the shadows of the road, that awful scream rang out once more:

"SCHEEEEEIIIIIF!"

It pierced the air like a siren, echoing off the trees and tearing through the silence.

The car jolted and swayed as Kyle pressed the gas harder, speeding down the trail. Misty was gripping the dashboard with one hand, pressing her sleeve against her bleeding arm with the other. Her breaths came fast and shallow.

"He's still coming!" she cried. "Kyle, he's running—he's *keeping up!*"

Kyle checked the rearview mirror—and almost wished he hadn't.

In the red glow of the taillights, **a shape moved**, lurching unnaturally fast through the trees. Arms swung low. A pale blur of a face came in and out of sight as it veered alongside the car, never falling behind.

It was like he didn't feel gravity. Like something broken was propelling him forward.

"Faster—!" Misty cried.

Kyle pushed the car to forty, then fifty. The Nova's engine groaned with the effort, suspension creaking as they bounced over old roots and stones. The road curved sharply ahead, and Kyle swung the wheel hard, the tires slipping, nearly sending them into a ditch.

Misty turned to look behind again.

That sound came back, **scraping**, like nails along the body of the car.

Then—**THUNK.**

The whole vehicle jolted. Misty screamed again.

Schief had reached the bumper.

Kyle gritted his teeth. "I'm not stopping!"

The speedometer hit sixty.

The car's rear bucked again as weight shifted onto it. Kyle looked in the mirror and saw a flash of movement—claws dragging down the trunk, leaving long, ugly grooves behind.

Then, for a moment too long, Schief's face appeared once more in the broken rear window. Close. Watching.

He mouthed the names again.

"Sssschiiieeff... Mmmissschyyy..."

The claws slammed down—twice, carving into the metal. The car jerked, the tires kicking up gravel.

They were approaching a curve, and beyond it, the surface turned from dirt to old asphalt.

Kyle shouted, "Hang on—we're hitting pavement!"

The Nova surged forward, and with a final jolt, the car hit the blacktop hard. The tires squealed. The rear end skidded slightly—but the sudden surface shift was enough.

From behind came a scraping sound, then the slam of something hitting the ground and rolling.

Misty turned to look. She saw a flailing shape tumble wildly across the gravel and dirt, rolling and bouncing in violent arcs as if the road had thrown him off. But even as the taillights began to fade him into shadow, Schief was already moving.

He rose in one fluid, unnatural motion, arms dangling, legs bent oddly beneath him, then stood there, ragged and looming in the center of the road.

And then, he howled.

Not a word. Not a growl. A scream — primal, furious, full of agony and rage. His neck craned back, mouth wide, and from deep within his shattered chest came that name again:

"SCHIIIIIIIEEEEF!!"

The sound chased them down the road, impossibly loud, until it was drowned beneath the hum of tires on pavement and the frantic rhythm of their own breathing.

Kyle didn't stop. He didn't even look back.

They were alone again. Speeding down the empty road.

But the echo of that scream stayed with them.

The echo of that scream still clung to their ears long after it had faded. Kyle didn't let off the gas for several miles, gripping the wheel in a death-hold, his eyes flicking between the road and the mirror. Misty sat slumped in the seat beside him, arms wrapped tightly around herself, the sleeve of her jacket stained dark.

Neither of them spoke for a long time.

Only when they reached the blinking yellow caution light at the edge of town did Kyle ease his foot off the pedal.

The Nova rolled to a slow stop at the county sheriff's office—an aging brick building with one flickering overhead light and a porch that looked like it hadn't been swept since last fall. The town had downsized over the years. There were fewer deputies, and fewer people to protect.

Kyle killed the engine. The silence afterward was deafening.

They sat for a moment. Breathing. Shaking.

Misty spoke first, her voice raw and hollow. "We have to tell someone."

Kyle nodded, swallowing hard. "Yeah."

Inside, under the sterile glare of fluorescent lights, the world felt wrong in a new way. Too bright. Too clean. Like a hospital waiting room after a nightmare.

Deputy Melrose was the first to meet them. He took one look at their torn clothes, their bloodied sleeves and hollow eyes, and ushered them into the small interview room.

Sheriff Danner came in not long after—older, gray around the temples, his face lined with the permanent skepticism of a man who'd heard a few too many ghost stories from teenagers over the years.

Kyle did the talking.

He told them everything.

How they'd gone out to Lover's Lane. How Misty thought she heard something. How they were attacked by something that wasn't human. Something that called itself **Schief**.

He even told them about the claws. The face. The voice whispering names.

Danner took it all in without blinking. He scratched a note onto his pad, nodded once or twice, and then looked up with that practiced calm.

"You're saying this man... thing... broke into your car. On foot. Kept up with you at sixty miles per hour."

"Yes," Kyle said. "He was *on the car*. He clawed the trunk. He—he said Misty's name. He hissed it, like... like he knew her."

Misty flinched at that, her hands gripping the hem of her sleeve.

Danner set the notepad down. "Did either of you get a good look at his face?"

Kyle and Misty nodded in unison.

"He looked burned," Misty whispered. "And... sick. His skin was wrong. It looked... like it melted once and then hardened again."

Danner exhaled through his nose. "You ever hear of a place called Chief's Marine and Bait Shop?"

Kyle blinked. "That place that burned down? Years ago?"

"Eighteen years," Danner said. "Caught fire late one summer night. No one really knows how. Rumor was the old man running it went nuts. Started drinking weird stuff in the back shed. Chemicals. Boat fuel. Things you don't come back from."

Kyle glanced at Misty. "You think that was him?"

Danner leaned forward. "I think you're lucky to be alive."

He stood.

Deputy Melrose stepped back into the room. "Sir, we had an old report a few years ago. Teen couple thought they were being stalked out near the fire road. Didn't see anything, but the boy's truck had deep gouges down the side. No animals matched it."

Danner grunted.

"File it," he said. "And make sure their parents pick them up. No one should be out past sundown until we sort this."

Kyle stood slowly. "You believe us?"

Danner didn't answer right away.

Instead, he looked out the window, past the flickering porch light, toward the dark treeline in the distance.

"I've heard the name before," he said quietly. "Not for a long time. But yeah... I believe you saw something. What exactly, I can't say."

Misty shivered and leaned into Kyle.

Danner finally turned to face them again.

"But if that thing is still out there—don't think it's done with you."

Hours passed.

Eventually, Misty's parents arrived, their faces pale, caught between relief and fear. Kyle's father came shortly after, gripping his son's shoulder tightly but saying little. No one knew how to talk about what had happened.

They were told to get some rest. The sheriff said he'd file a report, check the woods in the morning. Maybe even send someone from Fish & Wildlife.

But they all knew that wouldn't matter.

The thing that chased them, the thing that whispered names and carved steel like soft bark, wouldn't be found with flashlights or tranquilizer darts.

It wasn't an animal.

It wasn't even a man anymore.

Later that night, after showers and wounds cleaned with trembling hands, Misty lay awake in her bedroom, staring at the ceiling. Every creak of the house made her flinch. Every distant rustle outside drew her gaze to the window.

She could still hear him.

Not the scream, though that echoed in her dreams. No, it was the softer sound, the one that had crawled into her bones:

"Ssschiiieefff... Mmmissschyyy..."

She didn't know how he knew her name. She didn't know what he wanted.

But she knew he wasn't finished.

Across town, Kyle couldn't sleep either.

He sat on his back porch, wrapped in a blanket, a baseball bat resting across his knees. His shoulder still throbbed where the claws had scraped him. The lines weren't deep, but they burned like they had sunk further than skin.

He looked toward the woods.

Out there, somewhere, Schief was waiting.

He hadn't come to scare them.

He had come for something else.

Maybe revenge.

Maybe hunger.

Or maybe, and this thought chilled Kyle most, maybe **he didn't even know why he was doing it anymore**. Maybe he was driven by pain, instinct, a ghost of a purpose long since melted away with his skin.

The town would whisper about this night.

Just like they had whispered after the bait shop burned down. Just like they whispered after the other strange sightings, stories passed along under breath during late-night shifts and school parking lot hangouts.

And like all the other stories, this one would twist with time.

People would say it was a prank.

An exaggeration.

Maybe even a lie.

But in the heart of the Northwoods, where the trees still carried ash on the wind and the shadows moved just a little too freely, the truth lingered.

Somewhere, Schief was **dragging himself through the dark**, his long fingers curling into the dirt, whispering the only names he remembered through half-melted lips.

And he was still looking.

Still hunting.

Still calling.

"Ssschiiieeff... Mmmissschyyy..."

Chapter 24: Echoes from the Lake

The car's tires whispered over the cracked gravel road, sending up faint clouds of dust that settled like forgotten memories on the worn edges of the forest path. Towering pines stretched their dark limbs to the heavy sky, needles trembling in the drowsy summer breeze, each breath a quiet sigh that seemed to carry centuries of secrets.

Mike gripped the wheel, his knuckles pale, the steady thrum of the engine the only anchor to the fading world beyond the trees. Beside him, Laura stared through the windshield, eyes distant, absorbing the slow, deliberate quiet that pressed against the glass.

They had left Milwaukee behind, chasing silence, the kind that seeps into the bones and drapes the mind in shadow. The cabin, a friend's retreat tucked deep in the Northwoods, promised a refuge, a chance to breathe through the tight coil of tension they'd carried for too long.

At the forest's edge, the gravel path gave way to a narrow lane shrouded in moss and shaded by dense birch and cedar. A sagging gate marked the entrance to a small clearing where the cabin crouched low, half swallowed by the towering trees.

The sky hung heavy, slate-gray clouds stretched thin like fragile parchment, hinting at rain. A gust stirred the branches overhead, scattering dead leaves across the hood of the car, the faint rustle a whispered warning.

Mike killed the engine, the sudden silence a palpable weight. Gravel crunched under their boots as they stepped out, the air cool and damp, tinged with the sharp scent of cedar and earth. Somewhere close, the faint splash of a fish breaking the glassy lake surface echoed softly into the stillness.

The cabin door was ancient wood, its paint flaking and faded like dried petals. Mike reached out, fingers brushing against the cold metal latch. The door groaned open with a tired creak that seemed to stretch into the empty room beyond.

Inside, the air was thick with the musk of damp wood and something else, something faint and sour, buried beneath years of dust and smoke. Shadows pooled in the corners, the muted glow of a single oil lamp casting amber light across rough-hewn walls and a low stone hearth cold and empty. Faded photographs hung crooked on the walls, faces blurred and timeworn, watching from another age.

The kitchen bore the quiet residue of a meal long finished: a blackened cast-iron skillet, a chipped enamel mug, and a bottle of Door County wine drained to its last drop, tipped on its side like an offering. The scent of grilled trout still hung in the air, mingling with faint cedar smoke from the fire pit outside. A half-glass of bourbon—Mike's—sat forgotten on the windowsill, the amber catching the last of the oil lamp's flicker.

Their voices had grown quieter as evening deepened, the alcohol warming their blood, their laughter fading into tired sighs. They moved slowly, often touching, hands lingering longer than necessary, eyes holding just a moment too long. A fragile peace settled between them, like soft ash on cold stone.

Outside, the wind picked up. The forest whispered in tones nearly human, swaying branches scratching lightly against the cabin siding—S s s c r a t c h e s... like slow fingernails tracing secrets into wood. The air grew colder. Laura shivered.

Laura pulled her jacket tighter around her shoulders. The quiet pressed close, an unseen presence hanging in the stagnant air.

They climbed the narrow stairs, the boards groaning beneath each step. Upstairs, the bedroom was cool and dark except for the pale, ghostly glow of the full moon filtering through the sliding glass doors that opened onto the lake-facing patio.

Sheer curtains fluttered in the night breeze, fragile and shredded, like sails torn by storm and time. The screen door stood unlatched, swaying gently, a hollow invitation.

Mike lit another oil lamp. Its soft, flickering light painted long shadows, the quiet hum of static crackling from an old radio filling the corners of the room.

They undressed wordlessly, the weight of silence thick between them. Mike pulled the thin cotton blanket up to their waists and turned onto his side. Laura nestled close, resting her head on his chest, listening to the steady beat of his heart—slow and sure in the growing dark.

Outside, the forest breathed, a slow, shivering pulse of leaves and wind and the distant, mournful call of a loon echoing across the still lake.

Then, the air shifted. A sudden chill threaded through the room.

Laura stirred in sleep, a soft warmth upon her legs. Her eyes flickered open, hazy with dreams and shadows. She blinked, confused by the dampness clinging to her skin, the faint, sticky warmth that was wrong, unfamiliar.

Slowly, her gaze dropped downward.

The blanket was torn, shredded raggedly as if clawed apart. The sheer curtains were now shredded strips flapping wildly in the cold breeze like torn sails caught in a storm.

Wetness spread across her calves. Her skin pricked with pain beneath the tangled strands of sheet mixed with blood emanating from countless lacerations in their legs.

She gasped.

Mike awoke with a sudden, sharp breath.

Together, they saw it, silhouetted against the rising bone-white moon, framed by the fluttering ribbons of the shredded drapes sending strobe like shadows throughout the room.

There he stood before them, a name only spoken by locals, Schiefe.

His body was a nightmare made flesh.

Wild, ratted hair whipped in the chill wind, tangled and slick with lake muck. His face was a grotesque tapestry of decay and torment—pocked and scarred, translucent flesh stretched thin over bone, veins swollen and bursting like cracked cords beneath his skin. Tiny parasites writhed beneath the surface, worms burrowing endlessly into his flesh, pulsing with a sickly, oily sheen.

His breath came heavy, congested, wet rasping g u r g l e s that echoed in the dead silence of the night.

His long left arms hung awkwardly at his side. His right arm trembled overhead. His Two fingers, grotesquely elongated and tipped with claws, dripped blood that glistened faintly in the moonlight.

His eyes, pale and cataract-clouded, flicked between the broken curtains, searching.

A guttural, broken mumble slipped from cracked lips.

"Schiiieeeeffeeehhhh.. Laa... r a a... Wa i f f f..."

The sound twisted in the air like smoke from a dying flame—ragged, desperate, fractured.

Then, suddenly, the scream shattered the night—
"S C H I I I E E E F F F F F!!!"
Piercing. Shrill. Unbearable.
Laura screamed back.
Mike lunged.
They stumbled toward the master bathroom, throwing the door closed with a crash and sliding the lock tight.
Outside, Schief did not try the door.
Instead, he lowered his monstrous frame toward the cracked plaster wall beside it.
Clawing began.
Slow, deliberate.
The brittle plaster crumbled under his long, sharpened nails.
Behind the broken wall, pipes twisted and coiled.
Schief pressed his grotesque face close, eyes wide, peering through the gaps.
A wet hiss crawled through the pipes.
"Schief... Laaa... r a a... Wa i f f f..."
They caught a glimpse of the worm-riddled face, pale and raw.
His breath, a sick rasp, bubbled through the gaps.
They caught a fleeting glimpse of his worm-riddled face, pale and raw, pressed close against the jagged opening in the plaster wall. The sickly glow of the moonlight revealed every grotesque detail, the

twisted flesh where parasites writhed beneath his skin, twitching and burrowing like living nightmares.

From the gaps came a wet, rasping breath—sick and gurgling—bubbling through the narrow space like poison seeping from a wound.

Suddenly, a terrible, grinding ssssshhhhh shattered the fragile silence—Schief's long, jagged nails scraping against the cold metal pipes behind the wall. The sound was raw, as shredded metal ribbons peeling off the rusted steel under his claws.

Mike's heart slammed in his chest as the horrible noise scraped its way along the pipes. Laura's breath caught in a strangled sob. They exchanged panicked glances, eyes wide and frantic, frozen in terror as the creature hissed and drooled through the narrow gap.

His mouth—oh God, his mouth—was a hideous cavern of decay and rot. Thick, glistening slime dripped from cracked, yellowed teeth that looked ready to crumble. A parasite-infested, deformed tongue lashed about, gargling a wet, guttural hiss that sent chills crawling across their skin.

Then, with a terrible, wet slurp, he withdrew his face from the pipe opening and shifted toward the bathroom door.

A fresh, scratching noise began, this time against the wooden door. Sharp claws raked the surface, scraping with a relentless, planing sound as the wood was being peeled away. The sound tore through the air, reverberating through the small room.

Laura's fingers clenched Mike's arm, her nails digging into his skin. They could only stare in paralyzed horror, knowing without a doubt—he *would* get inside.

The scratching grew louder, more insistent. Panic surged through their veins like icy fire. Mike's breathing came quick and shallow. Laura's mouth was dry, her heart pounding so hard it echoed in

Mike's breathing came quick and shallow. Laura's mouth was dry, her heart pounding so hard it echoed in her ears like a thunderstorm. The *sh r a p n e d* sound of claws scraping the wood grated relentlessly, a sick rhythm of impending doom.

They pressed back against the bathroom wall, hands trembling, faces pale in the moonlight filtering through the cracked window.

Then—abruptly—the scratching stopped.

An eerie silence swallowed the room, thick and suffocating.

They could almost hear the forest itself holding its breath outside, waiting.

Seconds stretched like hours.

A faint, wet h i s s escaped from the door's edge.

"S c c c c c h i i e e f f f... L a a a a r a a... W a a a i f f f..."

The twisted whisper echoed, ragged and broken, seeping through the cracks with a dreadful longing.

Laura clutched Mike tighter, barely daring to breathe.

The night waited.

The silence was a dark, heavy weight pressing down on their chests. Time slowed to a cruel crawl, each heartbeat thudding painfully loud in the tiny bathroom. Their breaths came in shallow gasps, the air thick with the scent of m o i s t decay, like damp earth after a long rain mixed with something far fouler.

Mike's eyes darted around, searching desperately for anything they could use as a weapon. The small bathroom offered nothing but brittle, cracked porcelain and a rusted metal towel rack. His fingers trembled as they wrapped around the edge of the sink.

Suddenly, a soft *thump* echoed from beyond the door. Then another, slower, heavier.

Schief's weight pressed against the doorframe like a grotesque promise. His ragged claws scraped lightly at the wood, leaving thin gashes, splinters falling like dead leaves.

Laura's hands shook uncontrollably. "M-Mike... what if he..."

Before she could finish, the creature's voice slithered through the narrow crack beneath the door, a low, guttural murmur dripping with venomous despair:

"Laaaaarraaa... waaaaiiifff...

The sound was a sick lullaby, broken and ragged, pulling at something buried deep in her mind, something primal and terrifying.

Mike swallowed hard, forcing himself to speak. "We have to stay quiet. He can't know where we are."

Laura nodded, biting her lip so hard it bled. The s h a d e d silhouette outside the bathroom flickered against the broken window, a monstrous, twitching shape that never fully revealed itself.

The long silence returned. The wind outside moaned softly, carrying the distant call of a loon that suddenly felt mournful and hollow.

Minutes bled into eternity. Then, another sound.

A soft scratching at the base of the doorframe, slow and deliberate, as if Schief was testing every weakness, every inch, seeking an opening.

The floorboards creaked under his weight, a sick *s c r e e e e e e c h* of nails against wood, echoing in the confined space.

Laura whimpered. Mike squeezed her hand, his own voice barely above a whisper: "Stay with me. I'm not going to let him in."

A terrible thought gnawed at them both, how long before the door gave way? Before the wall shattered under those horrid claws? Before the nightmare became flesh in the room with them?

Suddenly, the scratching stopped, cut off, clean and unnatural." A heavy silence slammed down on the room, thick and suffocating.

No breathing. No movement.

Only the faint rustle of shattered curtains and the whisper of the wind outside.

Laura and Mike held their breath, frozen in place, hearts pounding so loud it felt like the walls themselves would shatter.

Time stretched, each second dragging like a heavy stone.

Their eyes remained fixed on the door, wide and unblinking, waiting for the next nightmare to erupt.

But nothing came.

The silence was worse, oppressive, waiting, as if the forest itself was holding its breath.

Help Arrives

The sheriff's cruiser rolled cautiously up the gravel drive, headlights cutting through fog that had settled low along the tree line. Behind it, a battered red EMS van bounced over the roots and ruts.

Sheriff Lane stepped out first. Broad-shouldered, gray-bearded, and silent. He had seen things before. Not like this. But things.

He raised a flashlight, the beam cutting through the trees.

The porch light was off. The front door stood ajar.

Behind him, the EMTs, Willa and Jones, shared a nervous glance. Willa muttered, "Did the dispatcher say screaming?"

Lane nodded once. "Screaming. Woman said something was in the house. Sounded like she was running."

They moved as a group up the porch steps.

Inside, the living room was empty. Overturned chair. Broken lamp. A spilled glass of bourbon soaked into the rug.

Lane moved slow, hand resting near the grip of his sidearm. He stepped over a tangle of curtain fabric, shredded and damp. His boot made a soft **squelch**.

The light from his flashlight tracked up the stairs. Smears. Thin lines along the wall. Not thick. Not like a stabbing or a fight. But **dragged**. Finger-width. Or claw-width.

He raised the radio. "Dispatch, I've got signs of forced entry. Possible injuries. Gonna need backup."

Willa called from the hallway. "Sheriff—back here!"

He found her outside the bathroom door.

Inside, Laura and Mike sat on the floor, eyes wide, clutching each other like lifelines. Laura was shaking violently, her voice stuck in her throat. Mike managed a wordless nod, staring past Lane into nothing.

Jones knelt beside them, checking vitals. "lacerations. Shock. Hypothermic. No punctures. They're lucky."

Sheriff Lane scanned the bathroom wall. The drywall above the sink was **gouged**. Torn open like a wound. Pipes exposed. Small curls of plaster on the floor.

He moved closer.

Something had scraped through.

Not punched. Not broken with force.

Clawed.

And through the exposed gap… was the faintest trace of rot. A smell like water that had sat too long in a grave.

Lane turned to Laura.

Her lips trembled as she finally whispered: "He was in the wall…"

The Hospital

The sterile lights of the emergency room buzzed faintly overhead, casting a cold fluorescence that flattened the world into hard surfaces and quiet tension. Nurses moved briskly, wheeling carts, scribbling vitals, murmuring practiced reassurances that slipped past Laura and Mike without landing.

Laura sat on the edge of a padded gurney, her arms locked around her torso, fists clenching and unclenching as though her body didn't know how to be still anymore. Her hospital gown hung off one shoulder, exposing a line of bruises that were just beginning to bloom purple. Her eyes were hollow, rimmed red, focused somewhere no one else could see.

Mike stood nearby, one hand pressed flat against the window as rain traced thin lines down the glass. The outside world felt too ordinary, like it had never been breached, never been touched by the thing that now lived behind both of their eyes.

The doctor stepped in, clipboard in hand, his coat crisp, expression carefully neutral.

"You're both extremely fortunate," he said, flipping a page and scanning his notes. "Vitals are stable. No internal injuries. No fractures or organ trauma. But the lacerations on your legs are extensive."

He paused and looked up, as if trying to assess whether they were truly listening. Mike didn't turn. Laura didn't blink.

"Most of the wounds are superficial, surface-level cuts likely caused by sharp edges or claws. But several are deep enough that we had to suture in layers. There was some bleeding, though nothing arterial."

He shifted on his feet. There was a tension in his voice now, a hesitation that hadn't been there before.

"What's more concerning is the infection rate. Some of these wounds were already showing signs of necrotic inflammation when you were admitted. That sort of progression would usually take days. We're culturing samples, but preliminarily... it doesn't match common environmental bacteria."

He cleared his throat.

"To be safe, you've both been started on a broad-spectrum IV antibiotic—cefepime—and we'll reassess based on the cultures. Bloodwork looks clean, no systemic infection yet. But I'd like to keep you under observation for at least twenty-four hours."

Laura nodded absently, her gaze now trained on a scuff mark on the floor. Her voice, when it came, was flat.

"And the thing that did it?"

The doctor didn't answer immediately. He adjusted his glasses and gave a noncommittal shrug.

"We can't say for certain what caused the injuries. There's no clear bite pattern, and no venom traces in the wounds. Not a known animal. Nothing native."

That silence again. Not the comforting kind.

"But emotionally," he continued, more gently now, "you've clearly undergone a trauma response. What you're experiencing—numbness, fear, confusion— that's normal. Acute stress reactions often follow attacks like this. We can connect you with crisis counseling while you're here."

Mike finally turned from the window, his expression unreadable. "Will we ever be normal again?"

The doctor held his gaze. It was the first time he looked directly at either of them like a man, not a physician. His voice dropped.

"I don't know what normal means after something like this. But with help... with time... it can get better."

He set the clipboard down quietly and left the room.

The Broken Silence

Returning to their Milwaukee apartment felt like stepping into a life that no longer belonged to them. The air was too clean. The walls too white. The fridge still hummed, and the radiator still clanked at night, but the world outside had kept moving, oblivious to the fact that something had followed them home.

The silence that once felt like comfort now pressed between them like a third presence, an unspoken witness to the thing they wouldn't name.

Mike unpacked slowly, folding clothes with mechanical precision, as though the act itself could pin the edges of his unraveling mind back together. Laura watched him from the couch, her arms wrapped tightly around her knees. She hadn't spoken in hours. Her eyes were bruised with exhaustion, but she didn't sleep anymore, only drifted, surfacing and sinking through a restless gray fog.

The bed was no longer a place for sleep. They both avoided it. Mike took to lying on the floor near the window. Laura curled on the couch, always with her back to the room, as though turning her face to the wall could keep the dark from creeping in.

Sometimes she would startle awake in the middle of the night, convinced she'd heard something behind the drywall, a faint hiss, a dragging scrape, the sound of wet breath echoing through copper pipes. Other times, she didn't sleep at all.

Mike had grown quieter too, retreating deeper into himself with each passing day. He stared for hours at the hallway beyond their bedroom, his eyes fixed on nothing. More than once, Laura found him gripping the edge of the kitchen sink, unmoving, his knuckles white, as if holding on to something only he could see.

They didn't argue. They didn't talk. They moved around each other like shadows cast in different directions, tethered by memory but isolated by the weight of what they now carried in their minds.

The scrape of utensils on plates, the hush of running water, the whisper of a door shutting, these became their vocabulary. Not words.

Even the smallest sounds took on a sharpened quality. A creaking floorboard. The groan of a pipe expanding in the walls. Each noise was suspect. Each silence, loaded.

The distance between them wasn't measured in feet or time, it was measured in things unsaid. In glances quickly averted. In hands that no longer reached for one another at night.

And still, neither of them dared speak his name.

One evening, Laura sat motionless on the edge of the bathtub, fully clothed, the shower running behind her. Steam filled the room, beading on the mirror, fogging the walls. She didn't know how long she'd been there. Twenty minutes? An hour? It didn't matter. She hadn't felt warm since the cabin.

Across the apartment, Mike stood at the window, watching nothing. The city lights blurred in the wet glass like distant lanterns under water.

"I miss us," she said, her voice dry and brittle. A confession sent out into the fog.

Mike didn't turn. His fingers rested on the windowsill, motionless. "I don't know if we're still us."

The words hung there between them. Not an accusation. Not an answer. Just the truth, cracked open and left bleeding.

And still, the nights dragged on.

Weeks passed. Then months. The wounds on their legs eventually closed, but the skin healed wrong, tight, pale, and puckered like something had tried to claw its way out instead of in. The doctors called it scarring. Laura called it something else.

Neither one of them truly moved on. They simply adapted. Learned how to function around the holes.

Mike began sleeping again, but only with the bedroom light on. Laura placed towels under the bathroom door each night. They both kept the television on at low volume, even when they weren't watching. Noise was safer than silence. Silence invited him back.

Sometimes, in the middle of the night, Mike would jolt awake, sure he'd heard the hiss of his name in the heating vent. Laura would stand in the kitchen long after midnight, unmoving, one hand pressed to the wall as though trying to feel vibrations, scratching, crawling, breathing.

They never found mold in the walls. No pests. No rats.

But the smell returned sometimes, just faintly. A hint of damp rot, of something long drowned and dragged back to shore.

They never talked about it. Not anymore. There were no answers, and naming it only gave it shape.

They had escaped the woods. The cabin. The wall.

But Schief, had left something behind. A mark. A presence. An absence too large to ignore.

Not a haunting.

An echo.

And echoes don't fade. They repeat.

Chapter: 25 The Never-Ending Shadow

The harsh land of the Northwoods does not forget. It holds tight onto stories like a trapper's snare clings to its prey. Biting, deep, painful, unrelenting.

The landscape itself is etched with the echoes of those long-ago nights when Schief made himself known in the most brutal, visceral way possible. The woods hold those memories in the rustle of leaves, in the shifting shadows beneath the moonlight, in the mist that snakes across the quiet water before dawn. But this is not a peaceful calm; it is a silence born of something old and watchful. Something that waits.

Since the first stories began to circulate in the 1970s, the name Schief has been spoken in hushed tones, half in fear, half in disbelief. The creature, or whatever it is, has never been proven beyond the whispered rumors that flutter like dark moths from cabin to cabin, from town to town, through the thick pine forests of northern Wisconsin. The legend has become more than a story. It has become a pulse beneath the surface of the land itself. To those who live here, Schief is not merely a creature of flesh and bone. He is something more primal. Some say he is a curse laid upon the land, a deep-seated retribution for those that may be deserving of his wrath. Others whisper that he is the forest's own son, torn by broken dreams and pressing greed, a good man turned malevolent, from the quickly turning tides of life. And some completely dismiss the story as a fairytale born from drunks and fools.

The uncertainty only deepens the fear. For those that are certain that this is myth or fairytale, the wise would answer back that certainty is the lullaby we whisper to quiet the screaming of doubt.

Out there he watches, waits, and sometimes calls out, a piercing, bone-chilling scream that rattles through the pines and across the lake like a warning or a summons, the piercing, unmistakable cry of Schieeeefff. It shatters the quiet like a blade through glass, a sound that seems to emanate from the bowels of unthinkable nightmares. The shrill cry is said to echo for miles, carried on the wind to anyone foolish enough to listen. A scream in pain or a threatening warning?... Perhaps both.

But it is not only the sound that haunts the residents. It is the feeling that comes afterward. The heavy silence, the sudden drop in temperature, the sense that the very woods themselves have shifted. Dogs refuse to bark; children stop playing; grown men grip their weapons a little tighter.

Those who have lived here all their lives say the feeling never truly leaves. Visitors may chalk it up to superstition, or the isolation of a place where the woods stretch on forever, but the people who call this place home know better. There is a presence here, a cold something that watches from just beyond the tree line, that waits with patience too vast to comprehend. Its existence alone twists the air with a palpable tension. It is a presence felt in the marrow of the bones, an unshakable certainty that something unseen yet profoundly real watches just beyond the veil.

Schief was never just a figure of myth or local legend. He was real. The attacks in the '70s left scars that still throb in the collective memory of the community. Blood spilled into the forest floor and fed on by the very trees that then stared in silent witness and now stare down in complicity. The roots of the forest drink from that history, and the pines creak like they remember every scream. No rain, no raising tide can wash away the evil, the sins, the silent dread. A false innocence lost long ago.

Visitors sometimes arrive unaware of the dark reputation, drawn by the quiet beauty of the lakes and forests. They remark on the tranquility, the untouched wilderness, and then they notice the silence. No birdsong in the early morning. No rustling in the underbrush. No laughter echoing from campsites after dark. The remarkable absence of life after dark in the otherwise charming town. Instead, an oppressive stillness, a watchful pause that sets their nerves on edge.

Some leave early with stories of fleeting shadows and strange sounds; others never speak of their experience at all. There have been accounts of those that dared to venture deep into the woods at night, and never returned. Some have emerged from the woods torn with physical wounds, but more notably, the deep, permanent psychological devastation lingers long after the physical scars have healed. Hollow eyed. Silent. Forever touched. Forever ruined. What they saw or felt buried itself in their minds like thorns. Some speak in fragments; others never speak again.

The man, the creature, seems to exist just beyond the reach, an anomaly outside the normal rules of the world. In a way, he is part of the forest, a living shadow. Some say he bends reality, blurs the edges of perception, making those who see him question what is real and what is nightmare. After all, such things don't exist in the realms of reality, do they?

The townspeople have learned not to chase the legend. The wise elders advise caution, respect for the unseen forces that dwell in the woods. They warn that Schief is patient and always returns, and when he does, he does not forgive or forget. The silence that falls after his screams is the silence of waiting, for the next victim, the next chapter in a story that never truly ends.

The town itself feels different because of him. There is a collective breath held in the community, a shared understanding that the shadows belong not only to the forest. It is a dread that seeps into the very fabric of daily life. Children grow up hearing the stories; the fear becomes woven into their identity, a shroud they wear even as they laugh and play beneath the summer sun. He is alive in the woods and in their minds.

Even those who move away carry the weight of the legend. They say you can never truly escape Schief. The Northwoods call back, whispering in dreams and restless nights. The chill that clings to the skin when you least expect it, the sudden rush of wind through a quiet room, these are reminders that Schief is out there, watching, waiting, calling, eternal.

The End

Author's Note: The Story Behind the Shadow

I created the legend of Schief years ago as a young man, sitting around campfires while camping in the Northwoods. Though the story is a work of my own imagination, the reaction from those who heard it was unmistakably real, faces would tighten, eyes widen, and a hush would fall over the crowd like a living thing.

Over time, the story grew beyond its origin, taking on a life of its own in the minds of listeners. Now, after years of carrying it with me, I've finally put it on paper to share with you.

Schief isn't just a story about a creature lurking in the woods. It's about the feeling that some shadows, real or imagined, can cling to us, shaping the way we see the world around us. Whether you believe in the legend or not, I hope you'll feel the pulse beneath the silence and understand why this tale has never quite left me.

Thank you for joining me on this journey into the never-ending shadow.

— Anthony DiCristofano